I0748486

Thompsonville Collection

Mystic Song of The Deep South

Otis Windham Jr

Copyright © 2015 Otis Windham Jr.
All rights reserved.
ISBN Paperback 978-0-9998406-9-6
Hardback 978-1-7332382-0-5

Thompsonville Collection

Mystic Song of The Deep South

Otis Windham Jr

Williams & King Publishers

DEDICATION

This work is dedicated to MJJT, LJTWB, RHJ, MWA, EJW, NDC, JTP, JMA, AS and MM. Without your help and encouragement, this work would not have been possible.

PREFACE

Life has always had a unique flavor in the South. Everyday problems common to people in many other places give rise to different solutions in the all-Black town of Thompsonville. Thompsonville is an unassuming Mississippi town situated in the southern piney-wooded hill country. Louisiana is not too far to its south and the Alabama state line is much closer to the east. Thompsonville has an unusual heritage. It was established in the late 1800s by Georgia plantation slaves who migrated there during the Reconstruction. It has secrets and stories to tell about ordinary and not so ordinary people. Theseof love, happiness, fear, losing, winning, anger and sometimes sadness.

Thompsonville is indeed a "power place". Its people are, for the most part, good-hearted humble folk who respect, revere and enjoy a close connection to their heritage. Their lives reflect hope, never giving up and belief in a higher power.

"Thompsonville Collection, *Mystic Song of The Deep South*" is presented as a series of short stories with varied themes. Each story weaves threads of love, growth and transformation.

Otis Windham Jr

CONTENTS

DISCLAIMER

This is a work of fiction. Names, characters, businesses, places, events and incidents are either the products of the author's imagination or used in a fictitious manner. Any resemblance to actual persons, living or dead, or actual events is purely coincidental.

Written by Otis Windham Jr.

otiswindham2002@yahoo.com

Edited by

Anthony Smith

Category: African American Fiction, Mysticism, Southern fiction, Supernatural, fantasy

Otis Windham Jr

PRELUDE
(1854)

The days were shorter in autumn as the Georgia sun made its southward journey. There was a slight chill in the air as Dora Jane walked from her two-room cabin up the dirt path toward the plantation house.

"Massa Parker wants you up at Thompson House, Miz Dora," Sudie had come to tell her. Dora Jane, now in her eighty-seventh year, had spent most of her life as a slave on the Thompson Plantation in Georgia. She knew exactly what Parker Thompson wanted.

She was a "special" person. She had a perception of things most people were unaware of. Hers was indeed an unusual life. She had been afforded her personal quarters and more freedoms than the other plantation Negroes since she was forty-one years old. These freedoms were provided after Beauregard Thompson (her slave master) discovered she had a special gift.

"Aftnoon, Miz Dora," said little Amos as he passed her on

the path. The view of the Plantation House was magnificent as Dora Jane made her deliberate approach from the slave quarters. Her walk to the plantation house now took the better part of an hour. Age had slowed this once graceful specimen of humanity, but the gift she carried inside was still strong.

"Heah, Miz Dora, let me hep ya," spoke Enos the Butler as he came to assist her up the back steps to the large, white Plantation House. As she entered the kitchen, the smell of evening dinner overpowered her senses. Her body was old, and she was weary of the arduous life she had lived. She and Nero only had one daughter, Betty, who escaped up North after she gave birth to her second child. She left her mother (Dora Jane) to raise her daughters and never returned to get them. Dora Jane raised her grandchildren who were now grown and had grandchildren of their own. Though she had come to terms with her life, there was still something she knew she must do before she departed.

"Massa Parker," as he was called by the Negroes of Thompson Plantation, was its owner and Slaveholder. He inherited the estate from his father, Beauregard Thompson. Dora Jane had seen young Parker Thompson grow up on the plantation, go off to school to Harvard and then practice law in New York until his return to Georgia ten years ago.

Parker's time up north and his education had given him the skill and business knowledge necessary to move the Thompson Plantation to a higher level of profitability than it had ever known under his father. Though it was now a business success, that intangible something that had been this plantation's trademark was missing after its ownership passed from father to sons.

These years of rule by the young Thompsons had taken their toll on the Negroes of the Plantation. Even the white overseers, though none could put a finger on it, realized that the things that made this a special place to live and work were gone. Family units for slaves were no longer recognized or respected. The melodious singing, which echoed from the slave quarters at sunset, was no more. Discipline was now a cruel ordeal for those who ran afoul of the now strict plantation rules.

Parker and his younger brother Patrick were the only offspring of Beauregard and Lydia Thompson. Patrick, five years junior to Parker, had shown no aptitude or interest in mastering the business side of the plantation. He was not an educated man like his brother. He was, however, a tireless worker and a good overseer.

Beauregard Thompson had designated Parker to manage the Plantation at his demise. He knew Parker had the aptitude and the education to manage the business well.

Parker Thompson exercised none of the sensitivity of his father in managing the lives of those wretched souls who were so instrumental in the success of the plantation. He and his younger brother were not close however, he loved him despite his shortcomings. He felt much grief over his present situation. Patrick lay near death from the gunshot wound he received two Saturday nights ago outside Maxie's

Tavern. He was shot in a pistol fight with Randall McDuffie. He and Randall had never seen eye-to-eye about anything. Patrick was known to be a hothead when he drank. It was a miracle he hadn't been seriously injured or killed before now. The bullet was lodged in his chest and was too close to his heart to be removed without a high risk of certain death.

Patrick was Parker's only remaining living relation and if he did not survive this ordeal, Parker could possibly be the last Thompson of Thompson Plantation. Doc Fletcher had already told Parker there was nothing else he could do. The wound Patrick sustained was almost gangrenous and he was in constant pain when not sedated with the opiate mix Doc provided for him.

This dilemma forced Parker to do something he and Patrick swore they'd never do. He sent for Dora Jane; the old "Negress root woman." As he reflected, there was a knock on his study door and Enos appeared. "Massa Parker, Miz Dora Jane's downstairs in the kitchen," he said. Parker never gave the old Negro an acknowledging look. "Well, bring her upstairs," Parker said with no patience in his voice. He owned these Negroes, lock, stock and barrel, and felt no need to demonstrate any courtesies to them.

Parker didn't really believe the "rubbish" he had heard whispered about Dora Jane, but right now he was out of options. He knew it would only be a matter of time before Patrick succumbed to his injury.

He knew his Daddy and Mama had great faith in the old Negress, though he had never heard either say so publicly.

It was obvious, because they treated her so much better than the other slaves. Daddy even made provisions for her continued support and welfare in his will.

It was true that he couldn't recall that Daddy or Mama ever had any serious illness. They died together in the terrible fire that burned down the Southern Theatre in Augusta. He knew when they were alive, they believed Dora Jane was the reason for their continued health and well being.

As a child, he remembered when Daddy's friend, Billy Paine, was very sick with a strange fever and not expected to live. Daddy loaded Dora Jane in the wagon and took her with him to visit Billy. He recovered in less than a week and, to this day, still ran the Paine Plantation. Billy Paine made Parker numerous offers to buy Dora Jane after his father's death. Were it not explicitly stated in his father's will, he would have gladly accepted Billy's inflated price. Billy's offered price was three times what a childbearing Negress was worth.

Parker Thompson's learning and travels taught him a lot about the world, and he knew if God were to give the power to heal, to anyone, he certainly wouldn't give it to a nigger slave. Regardless, his love for his brother, who drank too much and consorted with the female slaves and generally led a pretty sinful life, forced him to this decision.

At that moment, Enos entered the study followed by Dora Jane. Everybody on the Plantation, including his parents, called her "Miz Dora Jane," Parker thought to himself. Imagine that. Why would any white person give any nigger slave that kind of respect?

"Come on in Dora Jane," said Parker in a subdued but authoritative tone. "I'm sure you heard what happened to Patrick. Doc Fletcher said he's done all he can and the best we can do is make him comfortable until the end comes." He stood up and walked around the desk. His tall stature and mutton chop sideburns cut an imposing figure as he towered over the small, frail aged Black woman. He looked up and away as he spoke, "I can't say that I believe anyone other than God himself, much less a Nigra slave such as yourself, can heal anyone."

His hubris belied a brief look of pain and desperation as he said, "Patrick is all the family I have left and he's in a lot of pain and suffering. See if you can do anything to help him, even if it's only to make his transition peaceful." With that, he turned his back and the air of privilege and superiority returned.

"I be glad to do what I can Massa Parker," said Dora Jane. She knew a Negro in this rugged new country had to be shrewd. They could never let their Master know they knew more than the Master thought they knew.

In Dora's mind, both of the Thompson sons together did not equal half the man their father had been. One son thought he was better because he could turn a greater profit using the new agricultural techniques and working his slaves harder. The other knew he would never measure up and thus found himself lost in a sinful and an abusive pattern that only brought pain to himself and those around him.

Neither Parker nor Patrick were married. Parker had once been, but was shamed when his wife left him to move out west with her younger lover, another promising New York lawyer. It was said she left Parker because he was impotent. After five years of marriage, they were unable to conceive children. It was said she was visibly pregnant with the young lawyer's child when they departed New York for San Francisco.

On the other hand, Patrick spent much time in the slave quarters after dark. This was common knowledge and the source of much gossip in the local community. Because of this fact, most eligible white women no longer considered him a good catch. He had produced at least two offspring in the slave quarters, though neither he, Parker nor the state of Georgia would ever consider either legal heirs to the Thompson estate.

"Enos, take Dora Jane to Patrick's room," said Parker in a less than hopeful voice. Enos proceeded to lead Dora Jane to Patrick's room.

The room was dark except for the small kerosene lamp placed by the bed. Patrick's pale face appeared almost vacant of life, as the light from the lamp reflected from it. He was easier the more handsome of the Thompson brothers. Dora Jane could see why Sudie and some of the other slave girls were attracted to him. He was normally a clean-shaven man, but his face now showed a week of beard growth. "You can leave now Enos," Dora Jane told him.

Patrick was in a bad way. Without intervention, his

remaining time on Earth could only be measured in hours. She looked at his wound. It was high on the left side of his chest and since Doc Fletcher was unable to remove the bullet, his entire left side was badly swollen and discolored. She touched his forehead with her wrinkled black hand. Though it was barely perceptible, she could feel what remained of his life's energy.

At that moment, Dora Jane assumed a healing position next to Patrick's bed. She closed her eyes and with both hands firmly clasped together, she began the barely audible chant she learned so many summers ago in the West African bush. Her chant had a subtle yet rhythmic refrain. It possessed a familiar yet strange timbre. It rose to a rich and vibrant pitch and filled the room.

"You must see in your mind," the spirits had told her. She imagined Patrick's physical image strong and healthy in her mind's eye. This visual image was surrounded by a pure white light which was whiter than one could imagine. This light was the source of the healing power that flowed through Dora Jane.

Patrick's image became clearer and more defined as the light surrounded him. Dora felt the spiritual force slowly carry her to a level so intense it has no description.

After what seemed like eternity, color began to replace the paleness of Patrick's countenance. Expression returned to his features as healing energy began to flow through him. It was sometimes said that Dora Jane's healings cured not just the body but also the mind.

Patrick's father (Beauregard Thompson), was a changed man after Dora Jane healed the severely broken arm, he sustained when he fell from his horse during the winter of his fortieth year. Before she healed him, Doc Fletcher had been ready to amputate his arm. After that incident, things were dramatically different for Dora Jane and the slaves of Thompson Plantation. After his accident, Beauregard's friends actually accused him of softness relative to his treatment of his slaves.

The swelling in Patrick's chest region had now subsided substantially. There was still some discoloration, but only a ruby red mark about the size of a plum remained where the gunshot wound had been. The paleness was gone from his skin and his breathing took on a stronger and healthier pattern. Dora Jane placed both hands on the mark left by the wound. She grasped it as if plucking a precious egg from a bird's nest. It was there glowing and contained in her hand. She squeezed it until all that remained was a red puff of smoke which rose slowly to the ceiling as it dissipated. Pink and healthy pink skin remained where the gunshot wound had been.

At that instant, Patrick bolted upright in bed, fully conscious with an urgent and puzzled facial expression. This reaction prompted Dora Jane to calmly lay her hand on his forehead and say, "Jus relax Massa Patrick. You come back from a long, long journey. Now jus lay back and rest."

Her healing hand and soothing tone instantly relieved his anxiety. He laid back and fell quickly into a deep sleep.

Though Patrick Thompson, as Overseer, had been the oppressor of every slave on the Thompson Plantation, he was still a child of God to Dora Jane. In his hour of suffering and need, her love was as great for him as it was for the little Black babies who were brought to her with blindness or some other birth malady. She held no animosity toward her masters for their judgment would come from on high. She also knew God had a special role for her in His plan.

Patrick Thompson's healing brought many changes for the Thompson Plantation. There was a good feeling there again. He no longer frequented the slave quarters or stayed late in the village saloons.

Two years after his healing, Patrick married Elsie Paine, the youngest of the Paine girls. This marriage quickly produced two male heirs to the Thompson estate. After Patrick's miraculous recovery, his older brother Parker had been forced to believe in the power of Dora Jane. Negro or not she had, through healing him, given Parker back the hope he had lost.

Dora Jane healed Patrick's injury and cured him of his base desires and his hell-raising lifestyle. In Parker's mind, it could only have been Dora Jane because people just didn't have the power to change on their own; not without some divine intervention.

Years later, one evening after supper, Parker Thompson quietly walked down the path to Dora Jane's cabin. He knocked on her door and her frail voice invited him in. "Miss Dora," he humbly asked after he entered, "Can you heal my condition?" Dora Jane, who was now in her nineties already knew what he meant; his impotence. "Les see," she said. "Open yo shirt."

Parker obediently obliged. Dora Jane was silent for a moment. Then she prayed and placed her dark and wrinkled hands on his chest. Parker could feel potent energy flow within him he had never felt before. He felt vibrant and virile. He knew in that brief instant Dora Jane's hands had cured him of his manly shortcoming. She then offered some advice to her Master. "Miz Mary Adams would probly be mighty pleased if you came a courtin," she said.

Mary was Parker's childhood sweetheart who had never married. She was thirty-eight and still a beautiful and fertile woman, though most people considered her a spinster. Some people thought she had waited all these years for Parker. He had been reluctant to court any woman because of the tragic emotional loss he still felt from his failed marriage.

He was overcome with emotion after the healing Dora Jane had given him. He removed a legal document from his coat and gave it to Dora. He spoke with much guilt in his voice. "Miz Dora, here is the deed to land in Mississippi that my father left to you in his will. He believed that one day all slaves would be free and he thought enough of you to leave this land for you and yours to start anew. In my selfishness, I was not going to give it to you."

Dora Jane was overcome by the generosity of the gift. She had tears in her eyes as she thankfully accepted what Massa

Beauregard had left for her. She knew this gift from Beauregard Thompson would provide her kin a better opportunity for many years. A year after Parker's visit to Dora Jane, he and Mary Adams were indeed married.

Another season saw the sun setting on Dora Jane's life. Her granddaughters, Helen and Ruth, were present with her in her cabin as she neared her end.

Though weak, she spoke, "Ruth the deed to the land Massa Beauregard lef me is on dat table. My time's most done. I been heah a long time and always tried to do God's will. My man, Nero is waitin for me jest on the other side." Nero was Helen and Ruth's grandfather who had left the plantation before either were born.

Nero escaped from the Thompson Plantation when Helen and Ruth's mother Betty was only two. Dora Jane never heard from him again. Dora Jane knew in her heart, if he had been still alive, he would have come back to get his family. She still loved him and never took another man after he left.

"I see tough times comin, but I also see a better life for you and yourn in Mississippi on this land Massa Beauregard give us." Both women looked sadly at their grandmother, but neither spoke. In her weakened condition she continued, "God didn't gimme my gifts for no reason. Yo chullun's chullun and their kin will also have the gift. One day the world's gonna see and be thankful for the gifts God gave us. We mus keep our feet on the path that has been set for us.

We must always look to be wise, keep love in our hearts, and try to do the Lord's will."

With those last words, Dora Jane closed her eyes for the last time. She had nearly finished her ninety-fourth year on Earth.

Georgia had never witnessed a funeral for a Negro slave as was given to Dora Jane. She left behind two granddaughters, Helen and Ruth, six great-grandchildren and three great-great-grandchildren.

She was eulogized the following spring afternoon by Reverend Sam, the slave lay preacher. Parker, Patrick, the Paines and some other White families were in attendance, in addition to most of the slave population of Thompson Plantation. Her body was laid to rest in a plain white dress in a shiny mahogany coffin. She was buried in the Thompson Cemetery very near where Beauregard and Lydia Thompson were laid to rest. As whites and Blacks paid their respects, few tears were shed. This was the celebration of the homecoming for a very special soul.

That beautiful spring day, just outside human perception, the soul of Dora Jane had taken on its spiritual body and was witness to the last rites of her life on Earth. Many lives had been touched and made whole by her kindness and healing hands. She had passed the difficult test and was now moving on to a greater glory. She was able to see the path her offspring would take. Her offspring would add much to the quality of human kind's experience on Earth.

She also had the opportunity to look back, as most souls do, and feel the burden lifted and view the rugged path it would never need travel again. Her spirit freed itself from its earthly body and moved upward. She took the waiting outstretched hand of her man, Nero, and their spirits disappeared together into the light.

LIAR'S HELL
(1949)

The army green 1947 Packard rolled into Thompsonville as the summer sun was directly overhead. The driver's face reflected that air of privilege and superiority of the southern White man in nineteen forty nine, Mississippi. Arthur Lee Landrum was born and raised in Jefferson County. He had been out of Mississippi just twice in his life, but that didn't make him a dim-witted peckerwood. His business office was located in Brewton, the Ku Klux Klan Capital of the New South. He was the only insurance agent for Georgia Life in Southeast Mississippi.

Well, Thompsonville didn't look a whole lot different from any other small Mississippi town. There was, however, a noticeable exception. The town was all-Colored or Negro as they now wanted to be called. Arthur Lee parked on Main Street and walked toward the General Store. These people seemed honest and hard working and appeared to have a very prosperous town for these times; better than many of the other towns where he sold insurance.

Arthur Lee normally went west on his routes. Though he had accounts as far north as Jackson, he lived only ten miles from Thompsonville's city limits. He normally kept his distance from this place like his other good White neighbors. He finally had a realization one day. "Why spend all of his time working poor redneck towns and ignore a fairly prosperous large community in his own back yard?"

As he walked toward the store an old colored man passed him and spoke. "Afternoon sir," the man said. He had to be at least seventy years old. Artur Lee gave the minimal respect White men usually gave to colored men who were up in age. "How are you doin' today Uncle?"

The man nodded and walked on up the sidewalk. If Arthur Lee didn't know any better, he would have thought that Nigger was insulted by his greeting. He wiped the sweat from his red face and walked into the store. He was easily fifty pounds overweight, but extra weight indicated health and prosperity in these times. He was lucky to have avoided tuberculosis when he was a kid. It was almost epidemic in Brewton and other places in the south during his childhood. For that reason, some obesity was not frowned upon during these times.

As Arthur Lee entered the store, the storekeeper was busy sweeping the floor. It was a neat place with an ample supply of goods on its shelves and large quantities of staple supplies in barrels and large cans distributed about. Obviously this store supported a large farming community. The storekeeper looked up in mild surprise as the large White man entered the store. The Negro storekeeper was about fifty years-old with graying hair at his temples. He appeared to be a physically fit specimen. "Afternoon," Arthur Lee said.

"Afternoon," the Colored man replied. "How can I help you, sir?"

Harvey Johnson watched the portly White man enter Ezra Smith's store from the window of his office. Harvey was Thompsonville's Chief of Police. The town didn't get many Whites and when it did it usually spelled trouble. Harvey was Thompsonville's fourth Chief of Police in the town's history and by any standard, was a good city servant. He had been reelected twice and everyone knew why. He was adept at handling tough situations.

Harvey figured this man to be some kind of salesman. Whites just didn't come into Thompsonville unless there was a benefit for them in some way. Harvey was not born here, but he knew just about everything that went on in his town. Thompsonville was a good place for Black people to live in the south. It wasn't perfect by any means. The town had its share of domestic conflict, public drunkenness, fights at the local night spots and other disturbances. There was even a murder ten years ago, but all in all this community had been a good home for Harvey and his family.

Harvey wasn't the only person who observed Arthur Lee entering the Smith Store on Front Street. Leroy and Levi were two of the town toughs. They were both high school dropouts who frequented the Dew Drop Inn and played pool all day. Levi was the hard case. He had spent two years in reform school. Most people felt Leroy Thompson could be a clean cut young man without Levi's influence. Levi Smith moved to Thompsonville from Chicago when his mother, Sarah Thompson Smith died prematurely from acute alcoholism. She had been ill many years before her death. Levi grew up on the tough streets of Chicago's west side. After his mother's death left him an orphan, he was sent back to her hometown of Thompsonville. Her parents, Sam and Elsie Thompson, were both in their late seventies. They were aged and in declining health and were just not able to provide a young male child like Levi the direction he needed in his life.

After Chicago, the slowed down pace of Thompsonville did nothing to capture Levi's attention.

"Look at that White fat ass," Levi remarked to Leroy as Arthur Lee struggled to extricate himself from the Packard. Leroy nodded in agreement. Levi was the leader and Leroy was the follower. Harvey made a mental note as he watched the two eyeing the large white man enter Smith's store.

Even as the last patron exited the store, Arthur Lee continued his sales pitch to Ezra. "......be a heck-of-a thing to get sick for a long time or die without any way for your family to continue. I've got just the policy for you, Ezra. Do you have burial insurance?" Ezra listened intently to Arthur Lee and responded politely.

"Yes sir, I do have that for me and my family through Thompson's Funeral Home & Mortuary."

Arthur Lee was quick with his counter. "I can give y'all burial insurance and life insurance in one policy. Tell me what you're paying per week for your insurance."

Ezra was polite to the White man in his store but was obviously not really interested in his product. "Mr. Landrum, I'm not interested in changing my insurance right now. My family has bought insurance from Ben Thompson for now on thirty years. You might find most folks in this town probably feel the same way I do."

Not to be deterred, Arthur Lee continued his assault. "I can give you the same coverage for twenty five cents less a month than you're paying now," he shot back. That promise was always the clincher. He could even go to thirty less for basic coverage but most times he never had to. Just as he was pushing for the close, Harvey Johnson entered the store. "Afternoon Ezra," he tipped his hat. "Afternoon Sir," he tipped to Arthur Lee.

The sight of Harvey changed Arthur's Lee's demeanor completely. The sight of a large, well-muscled colored man with a badge and a gun on his hip was something he had never seen or even heard of in these parts. To say the least, it was visually intimidating to Arthur Lee.

Harvey coolly walked to the cooler and extracted an ice cold Cola. He opened it using the bottle opener on the cooler and walked back to the counter where the men were talking. They stopped their conversation since there was no longer the privacy to discuss such a personal matter as life insurance.

"Pretty hot out there today," Harvey stated after he took a long swig of the soda. He dropped his nickel on the counter to pay for the soda as he spoke.

Arthur Lee was taken aback by a Colored man of Harvey's size and presence who looked him squarely in the eye. "Sure is," Arthur Lee responded. His redden face betrayed his calm demeanor. He dropped his business card on Ezra counter and proceeded to leave the store. "If you change your mind gimme me a call at the number on that card. Good Day."

Both Ezra and Harvey looked amused as Arthur Lee waddled out the front door. "They'll do just about anything for a buck," Ezra commented. His tone was much different than it was to the White man. "Even come down to a community like ours to sell their worthless product," he continued. Harvey gave Ezra a puzzled look. "Heard about a Colored man up Yazoo City way who paid on a life insurance policy for thirty years. When he died, his widow presented his death certificate to Georgia Life and they never did pay the benefit. Hearsay they had to bury the man in a pine box. Nope. Not me. I won't be buying insurance from him and no other White folks," Ezra stated.

Harvey smiled, "You shouldn't judge everyone by one incident Ezra. Besides, you don't really know if that story is true or not."

Ezra looked a little grumpy. "I'm sure it is," he countered.

As Arthur Lee made his way back to his car, Levi and Leroy approached. "'Scuse me Suh. Could we speak to you a minute?"

Arthur Lee sized up the boys quickly. Levi's processed hair and pressed pants told Arthur Lee he was probably one of those young nigger city slicks. It was obvious Leroy was just a "want-a-be" country boy. These two didn't appear to represent any potential business to him.

"What can I do for you boys?" he asked.

Levi presented his offer. "We wonder if you might be looking for some entertainment?"

Arthur Lee was listening more intently now. "And what kind of entertainment did you have in mind?"

"Well Suh, there's some pretty gals down in the Bottom. We can get a date for you for a small fee."

Arthur Lee was thinking now. He had always heard "a man could change his luck by sleeping with a Colored woman". "And just what do you boys call a small fee?"

Leroy spoke for the first time. "Well, suh, five dollars for the gal and two dollars for us. For that small price you gets some good entertainment."

Arthur Lee was ever the Businessman. "And just what do

you boys do to earn a dollar a piece?"

Levi was quick to respond as it was now obvious Arthur Lee was interested in their proposition. "We'll look out for the girl's ole man. He's a little jealous, but he's at work at the mill till five o'clock. We can take you to her house."

Arthur Lee thought about the boys' proposition briefly and posed another question. "What does this girl look like? Does she have large breasts?"

Leroy fielded that question. "She is a nice size, suh. Her breasts is large and her bottom is round and sexy." He looked at them differently now. Arthur Lee thoughtfully contemplated the opportunity to change his luck by sleeping with a voluptuous Colored girl. "You boys get in," he said."

As he exited the store, Harvey watched the two boys get into the car with the large White man. He knew that meant trouble. The big Packard rolled down the street toward the Bottom.

Annie Sue Wells was a good-looking woman. She was twenty-three years old, but had already been married for four years. She married Tommy Wells shortly after they graduated high school. He was a handsome football hero for the Fighting Hornets and she was the prom queen. Tommy had a good job at the mill and he was a good provider, but she just needed more excitement than their marriage provided. That's why she took up with Levi. He was a year younger than she was but he was exciting. He was a city boy who was too big for this country town. Levi wasn't jealous like Tommy. He didn't mind her sleeping with other men. Besides, she gave all of the money she made to him anyway. When she and Levi had enough money saved, they were going to blow this place.

Tommy was not the sharpest knife in the drawer, but he almost caught Levi leaving out the back door one afternoon, when he and Annie Sue overslept after some serious lovemaking. Annie Sue didn't need a job. Tommy gave her enough money for the few things she could get in town.

"Hey baby, open up. It's me." Levi said.

Arthur Lee and Leroy watched as the door opened. A well-proportioned brown skinned woman came to the door.

"Step out on the porch so our customer can see what he's buying," Levi said.

Annie Sue stepped onto the porch and turned all the way around so the passengers in the car could get a glimpse. She wore a white blouse that accented her ample breasts and a tight-fitting skirt that showcased her cute bottom and shapely legs. As she reentered the shotgun house with Levi following, he motioned for Arthur Lee to come inside. Arthur Lee could hardly restrain himself as he got out of the vehicle and ran up the steps to the shotgun house.

A few moments later, Levi came out and walked down the steps to the car. He motioned for Leroy to get out. They walked down the street towards the pool hall. They shot pool and drank beer with the money Arthur Lee gave them till about 6:30pm. "Let's go over to Mae's Diner and see what the special is," Levi told Leroy.

As they walked through the Bottom, an uneasy look came over Levi's face. The cigarette he was smoking fell from his mouth to the ground. The Packard was still parked in front of Annie Sue's house along with Harvey Johnson's police cruiser and another official vehicle. Something had gone wrong. Levi knew Tommy got off at five o' clock. He was sitting at the dinner table by 5:30pm each day.

Leroy was also nervous about this very peculiar situation. "What you think happened?" he asked. "Don't know," Levi responded, "but we ought to put some distance between us and where we are right now." They turned the corner just before they passed Annie Sue's house and walked back toward Main Street.

Harvey looked first at Annie Sue, then at Tommy and then at the White man on the floor. The large dead White man on the floor. He scratched his head and asked again. "Okay Annie Sue, tell me again what happened here."

She was nervous, really nervous. Even though her husband Tommy was none too bright, Harvey knew him to be an honest, hard working man who thought the world of her. "It's like I said. He knocked on the door and said he was selling life insurance and asked if me and my husband would be interested in buying some. I told him I didn't think so. Then he said it was really hot outside and could he come in and get a glass of water. I let him in and when I got back with the water, he was face down on the living room floor choking and turning red. I went next door to Miss Mary's to use her telephone to call you. When I got back, he was still. Very still. I guess by then he was dead."

Some of what she said rang true, but some did not. Harvey observed Tommy hugging and comforting his wife. He was none the wiser. Poor kid. He was blinded by his love for her. Harvey motioned for Ned Adams to come outside to speak with him, in private. Ned served as coroner for Thompsonville. He was also the town's only doctor. Ned was a northerner who had moved to Mississippi after completing his internship in New York. He brought the town a service it sorely needed. He could have made much more money up north, but he was a man who felt service was more important than personal riches.

He was the kind of person Thompsonville was glad to take in and adopt as its own. The furrows on Ned's brow told Harvey something was amiss. "There are a couple of things that don't add up Harv. I believe he had a heart attack, but there were semen stains on his undershorts. I certainly didn't want to mention that in Tommy's presence. I also don't believe that's the location where he died either. I believe the body was possibly moved from the bedroom. Also, his undershirt is on backwards. Would a grown man do that himself? If I can see all of that with just a quick examination, what will the White County Coroner find? Harv, I'd say we got a real mess for ourselves here."

Harvey was deep in thought after Ned gave him this unwanted information. Ned was right. This was a problem. Although Harvey was Police Chief, he wouldn't get the respect a White Chief of Police would receive in this particular situation. This was a very delicate matter and would require some thought. He had already reported the incident to the Brewton authorities since the dead man had a Brewton address. It was just a matter of time before the repercussions began. His mind returned to the present. Harvey went back into the house to talk to Tommy and Annie Sue. "It's going to be a while before we get this situation cleaned up here Tommy, why don't you and Annie Sue grab some things and stay at your Momma's house tonight?"

"Sure, Chief Johnson. Come on baby, let's call Momma," said Tommy. Both were relieved (especially Annie Sue) and anxious to free themselves from the present ugly situation.

Harvey went back outside to speak to Ned. "Ned, there's nothing more for you to do here. Run along and I'll deal with the Brewton authorities when they get here."

Ned was agitated by his suggestion. "I don't think so Harvey. We both know the good White folks of Brewton aren't going to take this very well. Besides, I need to give my report to the Brewton authorities. I'll be here if there are any questions." Ned was a brave man and Harvey appreciated his dedication to his job and to him personally.

Just about the time Tommy and Annie Sue were out of sight, as they walked down the road to Tommy's mother's house, a caravan of police cruisers and official vehicles from the town of Brewton and Washington County arrived.

A big White man almost as large as Harvey, and just as well muscled, exited the first vehicle with a flashlight in his left hand a large pistol strapped to his right hip. There were five vehicles in all; three police cars, a vehicle with the county seal and a hearse. They stopped in the middle of the street blocking traffic in both directions. Four of the men wore uniforms. A crowd of black and brown faces was now starting to form. Ned and Harvey knew that here in the 1940's, in Mississippi, they would probably be short of help if an altercation ensued. The large man addressed his first comment to Harvey. "You Harvey Johnson?"

Harvey responded with professional courtesy. "Yes, I am. I'm the Chief of Police for Thompsonville. You must be Chief Wiggins." His confident demeanor got a little more of the group's attention.

"What happened here?" Chief Wiggins asked.

"It's just as I told you on the phone. It appears Mr. Landrum had a fatal heart attack. This is Ned Adams, our town's coroner. He's examined the body. "He's written a report for your medical people."

Ned handed the report to Sam Wiggins which he accepted but did not read. Sam was a mean man who wasn't going to take a lot of foolishness from the "Nigras" of this broke down coon-ass town, as it was referred to in Brewton. Sam called to a man standing behind him, "Wilford go inside and examine the body." A smallish White man with a medical bag left the group and went inside.

Levi and Leroy sat in Mae's Diner wolfing down the special. Today it was pork chops and collard greens. Mae personally waited on them, "You boys need any more iced tea?"

"No Mam" Leroy said. After she left Leroy posed a question to Levi. "You think that White man died or something?"

Levi was calmer about the situation than Leroy. "If Tommy came home and caught him in his bed… I'm sure that's what happened. Why are you so nervous? We didn't do anything. We don't have anything to worry about, so take it easy."

Levi's big city attitude about everything was somewhat disturbing to Leroy. Leroy was born and raised in the South and he had seen firsthand the violence *White folks* were capable of committing on innocent Colored people. He didn't really consider himself and Levi innocent since they were responsible for bringing the White man to Annie Sue's house.

The small group of White men were standing around smoking cigarettes and talking when Wilford, the Washington County coroner, came to the front door of the house. He motioned for Sam to come inside. Sam went inside and stayed for about ten minutes. They both exited together and continued to speak for a while. Sam Wiggins dropped his cigarette to the ground and crushed it with the heel of his boot. He then motioned to the hearse drivers. "Pick him up and take him back to Brewton," he told them. The two young attendants went inside with a stretcher to retrieve the body.

Sam Wiggins walked over to where Harvey and Ned were standing. He spoke arrogantly to Harvey. "Arthur Lee Landrum was a respected man in Brewton. Wilford showed me some pretty suspicious evidence on the body. Something about this whole situation stinks. Where is the gal that lives here? I want to question her."

Harvey drew the line at that even though he knew he was treading on thin ice. "This is my jurisdiction. I'll do the investigation. My call to you was only a professional courtesy. After the investigation, if I feel there was foul play, I will perform arrests and any suspects will be given due process by the Thompsonville Legal System."

The Colored crowd was even bigger and because both Sam and Harvey were talking loud, both sides of their conversation could be heard by all. By this time the deputies standing behind Sam were getting antsy. "Good White folks in Brewton ain't gonna take this sittin down. Looks like you folks just found yourself some trouble."

The attendants had just completed loading Arthur Lee's large body into the hearse. Sam Wiggins figured he would use the opportunity to exact justice. With all of the people standing around, now was not the time. He would also deal with that uppity nigger who was grandstanding behind the counterfeit badge he was wearing.

The biggest job he had to do now was telling Arthur Lee's wife he was dead. All the cars drove away (including a deputy driving Arthur Lee's Packard). As the crowd started to disperse, Ned's look of relief was halted by Harvey's words. "This is far from over. You and I both know what probably happened here and so does that crowd of thugs hiding behind badges. An excuse is all they need to perpetrate violence against someone they feel they have the odds against." Ned nodded his head in agreement.

As Harvey sat at the table in Mae's Diner, he saw Leroy and Levi, sitting in a booth near the window. They had just finished eating and were smoking cigarettes. As Mae brought his iced tea, Harvey picked up the ice-cold mason jar and walked over to where they were seated. He pulled up a chair in a position which made it difficult for either of them to get out. "Hi fellas," he said.

"Hi Chief," said Leroy.

"What can we do for you Suh?" asked Levi.

"No. It's what can I do for you. Look," Harvey's tone was very stern. "I know both of you know something about what happened to that White insurance man down in the Bottom this afternoon. Tell me and make it easy on yourself."

Levi set the tone. "We don't know nuthin. We was down at the pool hall all afternoon. Ain't that right Leroy?"

Harvey looked at Leroy. Perhaps there was something left to save in that one. "Tell me the truth Leroy. That man was from Brewton and you know how they think over there. This situation could be bad for the whole town."

Leroy squirmed. He was made very nervous by Harvey's questions, but did not concede. "We don't know nuthin. It's like Levi said, we was at the pool hall all afternoon."

Harvey picked up his tea and spoke directly to Leroy, "Leroy, you can do better as soon as you wake up and start to think for yourself. Mark my word, if you continue to hang with this one (nodding toward Levi), you'll come to a bad end." He went back to his table, finished his meal and walked back to the police station. Tonight could be a long night.

Harvey had two deputies who were both part time. Both were family men. Bob Johnson worked at the mill full time and worked evening shifts on Monday, Wednesday and Friday. Arthur Thompson was also a member of the Town's Fire Department and tonight was his shift at the fire station. This is what it took for men to raise families in these times.

They were blessed to even have jobs. A lot of the Colored folk in Jackson and the Delta had already started migrating north for jobs because times were so hard for Negroes in Mississippi.

The food at Mae's was good. This made it hard to keep one's eyes open after such a good spread. Harvey dozed in the chair briefly and was suddenly awakened by screeching tires on the pavement outside his office. He heard the report of guns, "BAM, BAM, BAM" as numerous vehicles sped down the street. Harvey looked out the window to see three vehicles full of white robed occupants with shotguns heading down the street toward the bottom. He grabbed his holster and handgun, got a rifle from the case and went outside to get into his cruiser to give chase. He was only one man and catching them could prove to be suicidal.

As he headed toward the car, some of the patrons of Mae's Diner were standing on the sidewalk watching the drama unfold. Mae approached him, "Harvey, you can't give chase to all dem Klansmen by yourself."

Harvey looked at her and continued to his car. "I'm the Chief of Police here, and if I don't who will?" he replied. He got into the cruiser and gave chase. He knew exactly where the caravan would stop. As he suspected they had stopped at Annie Sue and Tommy Wells' house in the Bottom. He cut his car lights off and stopped two blocks short of the house.

All of the men were hooded and dressed in Klan attire. Harvey saw the cross they had planted burning in the yard. Two men went inside the house and exited after a short while. Gunfire rang, "BAM, BAM, BAM" as they were outraged because no one was home. Eventually someone had the idea to burn down the house.

By that time Harvey had positioned himself behind the tree with a clear view of the yard. He was an excellent marksman. When a hooded man approached the house poised to throw a flaming torch, Harvey let go a barrage of gunfire. He moved and shot from all directions. The Klansmen were in a state of confusion. They didn't know how many people were shooting, or from which direction the shots came. In spite of all of the shooting, nobody was seriously hurt. The man with the torch dropped it on the ground as he ran toward a pickup truck. The group hastily loaded themselves back into their trucks and sped out of town swearing all the way. "We're gonna get you Niggers. Just wait and see!" somebody yelled.

Meanwhile, Levi and Leroy had left Mae's and returned to the pool hall. They were enjoying a game of pool. "Levi, I hear that peckerwood Chief of Police was pretty mad over at Annie Sue's house. I'll bet they gonna be lookin' for her and whoever she knows," said Leroy.

Levi was not fazed by Leroy's concern. "What you so scared of Leroy? What's wrong with your cotton-pickin' ass? Nobody saw us with that White man. And if they did, so what. We didn't do nothin wrong. Stop your worrying!" Leroy was not put at ease by his comments. Any time a White person died under suspicious circumstances around Colored folks, guess who had to prove they didn't have anything to do with it.

Leroy had a grave realization at that moment. Aunt Bessie had warned him numerous times he would come to no good end hanging with Levi. This situation was getting too tense for him. Besides, Annie Sue was Levi's woman, not his. Any trouble she was in with those Brewton rednecks didn't include him. Now was a good time to make his exit and try to get back on the straight and narrow. "Levi, I think I'm goin' in early tonight. I'll see you later." With that statement He put down his pool stick and made for the door. Neither man realized that would be the last time they would ever speak to each other again.

After stopping by the house to bathe and get a change of clothes, Harvey settled in to spend the night on his cot at the police station. Mary Beth understood the job he had required that sometimes. He expected the rest of the night to be quiet after the ruckus in the Bottom, but Harvey knew this issue was anything but over. He heard a faint knock on the office door just before it began to open. He knew from the sound of the knock who his late-night visitor was.

Levi lit a cigarette after he and Annie Sue finished their passionate lovemaking. "It's been so long Baby," she said. After all that mess the other day, I wasn't sure you were going to come back to see me."

Though she was older, Levi was the more mature of the two men in her life. That's why she liked him. He was much more of a man than Tommy. Tommy really was a mama's boy. If she had been able to see that in him, she never would have married him. "Now why would you think that? You know you're my number one." Levi inhaled deeply and blew the smoke from his nostrils. He then put the cigarette in Annie Sue's mouth. She took a deep drag. "You know it's pretty hot around here. I think I'll head back to Chicago a while till things get a little cooler," he continued.

Annie Sue looked hurt by his plan which didn't include her. "Levi we always talked about leaving this town together. Let's leave here, me and you, tonight. I can get a job wherever we go and we don't ever have to lay eyes on this place again."

He rolled his eyes to the ceiling and thought about her suggestion. "What about Tommy?" he asked.

"Don't think I'm stupid. You and most everybody in this town knows you're my man except Tommy. I want to be with you. I'll do anything for you."

Levi knew that would be her response. Why not take her. She was his moneymaker. She always gave him any money she made and some of what Tommy gave her. She told him how the fat insurance man had gotten over excited yesterday as she took off her clothes and he saw her beautiful body. His excitement must have caused some kind of seizure because he collapsed on the bed stark naked before he could even do anything. She struggled to put his clothes on and dragged his heavy body back into the living room. Then she called Chief Harvey Johnson. In her mind, she had gotten in all of that trouble for Levi. After all that, he couldn't possibly be thinking about leaving without her. Especially after she heard those White men had come back looking for her last night. All of this was for Levi. Certainly, he could see her agitation at his suggestion.

"Okay Baby, we got enough money saved to get us to Chicago. Pack a bag and meet me at the bus station tonight. We'll catch the nine o'clock Greyhound. I'll get the tickets. All you need to do is get away from Tommy and we'll blow this burg." That was more like it and exactly what Annie Sue had been waiting to hear him say.

It was two o'clock that hot July afternoon. The events of the previous day and night were far removed from their thoughts. As Levi slipped out the back door, he was careful, as always, to make sure no one was watching. Careful though he was, eyes were watching. The White hunter dressed in camouflage fatigues with the field glasses saw him make his exit. The face paint he wore minimized the sun's glare on his White face.

Annie Sue knew it would be easy to get away from Tommy tonight. He worked hard at the mill. After a large meal and a hot bath, they would sit and listen to the radio and Tommy would be asleep in the easy chair by 7:45pm. He would eventually get up and come to bed around midnight. It was the same thing almost every night. This would be the last night of that sorry, old, dull routine. She was excited about going away to the big city with Levi. Somehow, she felt Tommy would understand.

Harvey looked out the window of the police station. Today was hot just like yesterday. These parts of the Deep South were going through a real hot spell. Both Bob Smith and Art Thompson were on patrol, so he was at the office. He has asked them both to keep an eye on Tommy and Annie Sue Wells' place to make sure they didn't have a repeat of the previous night.

It was almost six in the evening and it was still hot. The ceiling fan did not pull much cool air through the open windows of the station. He wiped sweat from his brow with the white handkerchief from his back pocket. So far it was a quiet day.

He had not seen or heard any more from the authorities in Brewton regarding Arthur Lee Landrum's death. That's what was really strange. His buddy Russell had thrown some light on the situation for him. Harvey wasn't a superstitious man, but Russell Thompson was someone he listened to. Besides, Russell was a close friend. He would sometimes stop by on those evenings Harvey slept over at the Police Station. Harvey didn't grow up in Thompsonville however, he considered Russell a lifelong friend. He was one of the first people he met when he came to town. This place had an aura about it that was personified in Russell Thompson. He was the town's unofficial patriarch. Everybody respected him. He didn't give advice often, but when he did, it was listened to with few exceptions. Their conversation on the previous night provided some guidance to for him.

He didn't know how Russell knew what he knew, but he had that way of talking to you that made you feel comfortable. His advice always had meaning. His comment about the clandestine love affair between Annie Sue and Levi was precious. "Dwellers in forbidden shadows often inherit a Liar's Hell."

For these times, Russell seemed to be almost a saint. If he had vices he kept them secret from anyone around Thompsonville. He knew Russell to be a disciplined man. In Harvey's wife Mary Beth's opinion, Russell was a ruggedly good-looking man. As far as Harvey knew, he didn't have a woman in his life. His whole being seemed dedicated to the livelihood of this community. "Harvey, there is a calm before every storm. We'll weather this one like we've weathered all of the others," Russell assured him.

They spent many hours together at the lake catching fresh water trout, brim and catfish. They would have an occasional drink of peach wine together, play checkers and talk about many things just to pass the time, but a lot about Russell was actually still a mystery to Harvey.

It was now nightfall and the quietness surrounding Arthur Lee Landrum's suspicious death was deafening. Harvey had taken supper earlier at Mae's Diner with Bob Smith. The catfish special drew a large crowd on this night. Art was still on patrol and would stay so until Bob relieved him. Harvey would again sleep at the station until he was comfortable the Landrum issue had blown over.

A gentle summer rain began to fall as he made his walk at dusk from the diner to the station. He thought he recognized the woman sitting on the bench at the bus depot with the single piece of luggage. She looked the other way when he looked in her direction as if she didn't want to be seen. He looked at his pocket watch. It was 8:40pm. When he entered the station, he did not bother to turn on the single sixty-watt light in his office. He had a clear view of the bus depot from his office as he peered out the window. About 8:50pm, another familiar figure arrived. Harvey now recognized both figures to be Levi and Annie Sue. He saw that Levi also had a small bag as he passed what appeared to be a bus ticket to her. He lit a cigarette and looked nervously around in all directions as if he were expecting someone else to show. Harvey watched and was quite aware of what was going on. Levi and Annie Sue's relationship was almost public knowledge in the community and somehow he was sure he was not the only person observing this drama play itself out.

The bus arrived promptly at 9:02pm. Two passengers got off and the White bus driver punched Annie Sue and Levi's tickets as they boarded. The driver unloaded freight and luggage destined for Thompsonville, put on the Thompsonville luggage and re-boarded the bus.

Harvey had completed his assessment of Arthur Lee Landrum's death earlier in the day and mailed his official report to Jackson. There would be no further investigation by Thompsonville authorities, so Annie Sue was totally within her rights to leave town. As the bus pulled away, heading down Highway 27. He got into his patrol car. He knew his jurisdiction ended at Thompsonville's city limits however, he would follow the bus for a little while.

There was little traffic on the highway this night. After following the bus about five miles beyond the city limits, Harvey slowed to turn around and head back to Thompsonville. As he began his slowdown, he noticed the bus' brake lights illuminate suddenly and heard the screeching of its tires on the wet pavement. He abandoned his turn, cut off his patrol car's headlights and slowly proceeded to where the bus had stopped. Vehicles with bright lights and men in white Klan attire pointing shotguns and rifles blocked the bus' way.

He could see the men pointing guns at the Negro passengers who were forced to exit the bus. As Annie Sue and Levi stepped from the bus, a voice shouted loudly, "That's the Nigger Bitch and her man." Annie Sue screamed as two robed Klansmen dragged her, then Levi to the waiting vehicle. Levi tried to fight, but was hit in the head with a rifle butt. Harvey was helpless. He was only one man and the tactic he used last night would be suicidal in this situation.

He recognized the voice of one of the men as Sam Wiggins, the Brewton Chief of Police. He spoke to the three other Negroes who were forced off the bus. They were standing with their hands up looking frightened. "Y'all git back on the bus. We got who we want." Two men and a woman hurriedly reboarded the bus.

The hooded Klansman pointed his rifle, indicating to the bus driver to be on his way. The driver obliged and the bus started up the highway moving towards Brewton. Harvey, who was still watching from the woods, was startled by the sound of a twig breaking behind him. He drew his pistol and was surprised to see it was his friend Russell Thompson.

"Put that away, Harvey," he spoke. "We've got work to do." Harvey was mystified seeing Russell emerge from the dark woods so far from town. He didn't have time to question. They observed the Klansmen enter their vehicles and the caravan proceeded west on Highway 27.

Harvey and Russell followed at a safe distance. The group of cars all made a right turn down a dark red dirt country road. It was difficult for Russell and Harvey to follow the parade of vehicles down the narrow country road with the headlights off, but they continued slowly.

Two men against a mob intent on murder was a significant challenge. For some reason, Harvey felt comfort with his friend Russell Thompson at his side. He had often heard talk about Russell and some of the other Thompsons' strange ways. He wasn't sure. He had personally never witnessed any such thing and truly didn't believe most of the stuff he heard around Thompsonville. If Russell had anything to equalize this situation, now was the time to use it. Those two, Annie Sue and Levi, may have been morally wrong, but they had done nothing illegal and didn't deserve the fate the murderous mob intended for them.

The group of cars turned after going about a mile and a half into the woods and came to a large clearing. After the group parked, someone lit a large bonfire. It illuminated the forest as Annie Sue and Levi were both dragged from the car they were in. Both had their hands tied behind their backs and Levi's head was grossly swollen where he had been struck with the rifle butt. Blood stained his white shirt. Annie Sue's blouse was ripped and her ample bosom exposed, which seemed to further fuel the angry mob's passion.

The leader of the group spoke and quieted the angry crowd. "Bring 'em over here," he snarled. By this time, both Russell and Harvey were out of the car in the nearby woods close enough to hear. Harvey could feel the heat from the fire on his cheeks as the group proceeded to hold a mock trial for Annie Sue and Levi.

"You, gal are charged with the murder of Arthur Lee

Landrum, an upstanding resident of Washington County and Brewton, Mississippi," the leader pronounced. Then he looked at Levi. "And you boy, are guilty as her accomplice."

The fear in Levi erupted as a moan from deep in his throat. "Uhhhhh... please Suh, I didn't have anything to do wit dis."

Another angry voice bellowed from the crowd, "And this Nigger gal killed po Arthur Lee all by huhself. Is that what we 'sposed to believe?" he asked.

Annie Sue was crying uncontrollably as two Klansmen held her up and would not let her slumping body fall to the ground. The leader of the group removed his hood to reveal that he was indeed Brewton Police Chief Sam Wiggins. His racist arrogance did not allow him any fear of being identified by the frightened pair. His sinister smile looked even more menacing as the flames reflected from his face. "How do you plead gal?" he asked.

"Guilty!" proclaimed someone in the crowd.

Annie Sue fainted dead away at the pronouncement of her sentence. Her eyes rolled back into her head.

Sam then pointed an angry finger at Levi. "And you boy, how do you plead?"

Levi opened his mouth to plead, "Not guilty," but was hit again, this time in the mouth by a rifle butt before he could get the words out of his mouth. Blood and teeth splattered on the robes of the Klansmen who restrained him. Harvey could only wince as he witnessed this violent act.

Russell put his hand on Harvey's arm to prevent him from reaching for his revolver. He quietly spoke in an effort to calm him. "Let me handle it."

Harvey felt helpless, but something about the confidence in Russell's voice prevented him from committing an act he knew would get them both killed. He didn't know exactly what Russell had in mind, but his only choice was to give him an opportunity.

"This tribunal finds you both guilty as sin. Your sentence is to hang by the neck until you are dead". The terrible anger voiced by the crowd outpoured with yelling and gunshots at the verdict. Since two ropes were already draped over the large oak tree in the clearing it was obvious the sentence of death was a foregone conclusion. Sam knew if the verdict been anything other than "guilty", he would not have been able to prevent the angry mob from killing them anyway.

Both were taken and placed with hands tied behind their backs on barrels which stood underneath the nooses. A noose was placed around Levi's neck and the rope was drawn tight. Levi had to stand on his tiptoes to prevent his premature strangulation. Harvey was distraught and was not about to let this mob commit murder without a fight. He was puzzled that Russell still looked calm as he placed his hand again on his arm again to indicate it was not yet time to act.

As Annie Sue (who had come to and resigned herself to her fate) stood on the barrel, both of her breasts were now fully exposed to the crowd. Some members of the crowd got other ideas at the spectacle. "Hey, wait Sam" someone said. "We'd like to dish out some friendly punishment to this gal before we carry out her sentence."

Still another voice, "Yeah, I can see what got ole Arthur Lee all worked up." A man from the crowd loosed the rope and pulled Annie Sue from the barrel to the ground. Three more were on her as she fell to the ground. At that very moment, Russell walked into the clearing.

"Let her go!" he demanded. He stood bravely alone against thirty-five armed Klansmen. Harvey watched in horror as his friend Russell stood facing the angry mob. Levi looked in puzzlement. "Now what could Old Man Russell Thompson do by himself to save us?" he thought.

The men who were holding Annie Sue down on the ground released her and grabbed their guns. Annie Sue sat up and attempted to cover her breasts. She knew she could do nothing to prevent these men from raping her. At least Mr. Russell had bought her some time, but it looked like these angry men with all them guns were going to kill him real quick.

"Well lookey here," said Sam Wiggins. "Nigger, you must be crazy to walk in here alone." Russell looked him squarely in the eyes and spoke. "Let both of them go. They didn't kill Arthur Lee Landrum and you all know it."

The crowd was not impressed with his rebuttal. "The trial is over, these niggers have been found guilty and they will be executed," said Sam. "And we have had enough of your smart mouthing. Let him have it boys."

Gunfire rang out loudly. BANG!!! BANG!!! BAM!! BAM!! Smoke was everywhere. From his vantage point in the woods Harvey had his pistol drawn, but had to bury his head in the dirt as bullets and buckshot broke branches and ricocheted off trees and twigs all around him. Smoke was everywhere. Harvey was sure, along with everyone else, that this was the end of his good friend Russell Thompson.

When the smoke cleared, Sam Wiggins (his own pistol still smoking) looked up and Russell was nowhere to be seen. "I know we shot that nigger dead," said a high-pitched voice that broke the silence.

Even Harvey was wondering what happened. After a minute of silence, Russell's voice rang through the clearing from the opposite direction of where he was standing. "I said, let them go!!!"

This time, the tone of his voice struck surprise and fear in the hooded and robe-clad group. Sam Wiggins showed bravery the others did not. "I don't know how you got away Nigger, but we won't miss this time." BAM!! BAM!! BAM!!! The noise from the guns was again deafening as smoke once again covered the clearing.

Again, Russell was nowhere to be seen after the smoke cleared. "Sam Dammit, what kind of trick is that nigger playing?" A fearful voice uttered from the crowd.

Harvey was in awe from his vantage point at the ruse Russell was creating. "Over here," Russell said. He was again behind the shooting crowd.

"Ev Landry," Russell spoke loudly. "I'm talking to you!! You too Bob Davis. You boys are best buddies but Ev, did you know Bob is spending a lot of time at your house when you're not there?"

Both men removed their hoods in anger and surprise. Bob's face was red with anger. "Nigger, how did you know I was under this hood? Who told you all dem lies about me?"

Ev was now mad at Bob. He had long suspected just what the Nigger had said was true. Most of the crowd knew what Russell said was true, even though Ev only suspected it. "Bob, who you been tryin to git after? My little girl or my wife?" he asked. "I need to know."

The mob had lost interest in Russell, Annie Sue and Levi and were listening intently to the new drama being played out between Ev and Bob. Ev's pride and joy was his teenage daughter who had recently seemed to have taken quite an interest in men. "Both," said someone in the crowd and a nervous chuckle rolled through the crowd.

At that response, Ev Lunged at Bob and they wrestled around on the ground, kicking up dust, getting their white robes dirty, pulling out each other's hair and biting and scratching each other.

Sam Wiggins was pissed. He shot his pistol in the air - BAM, BAM. "Break it up!" he yelled. "Don't y'all see what he's trying to do? This Nigger can't possibly know that."

By now most of the mob had removed their hoods. "But we all know it's true," said Pete Smith. Russell then focused his attention at Sam Wiggins. "Your closet got some skeletons too, Chief."

The crowd became deathly quiet. Nobody had ever heard anything about Sam Wiggins. "Remember when you attended the Peace Officers convention in Jackson last year. Remember whose room......."

At that, Sam Wiggins loudly interrupted. "Alright Nigger, just what the hell do you want?"

When Sam posed that question it was obvious who now had control of this situation. Russell confidently walked around the crowd peering into the eyes of the men who were unmasked. He saw fear in each of their eyes. As he looked their way, each bowed their heads in fear of what he would do or say next. Sam Wiggins, however, was not about to go out that easy. Those other peckerwoods were fearful of this strange ass Nigger, but he would unmask their fears.

As Russell turned his back to Sam and continued his deliberate walk through the crowd, Sam drew his revolver, pointed it directly at the back of Russell's head and squeezed the trigger. The metal in the gun turned red hot. The hiss and the smell of Sam's flesh burning permeated the gathering. He dropped the pistol screamed and writhed on the ground. The racist mob was completely disheartened now. Here was their worst nightmare - "a Nigger who knew all of their business that they couldn't kill".

Some men were attending to Sam as Harvey slipped from his hiding place to free Levi and Annie Sue. The sight of

Russell's commanding and mystical presence moving confidently through the clearing erased the fear he felt for his life and the lives of the others.

Russell addressed the now disorganized mob and issued a warning. "Today is July 22, 1949. From this day forward if any of you ever seek to do harm to anyone from Thompsonville, there'll be some hell to pay. Arthur Lee Landrum was trying to change his luck. He changed it alright and if I ever see any of you in our town for that or any other reason, you'll get some of the same."

Annie Sue, Harvey and Levi were bug-eyed as Russell issued his warning. It was 1949 and neither had ever heard Colored folks talk to White folks like that. The warning Russell gave even sent chills down Harvey's spine.

"Now get the hell outta here and don't ever bother us again." Heads in the crowd were bobbing up and down as they picked up their hoods as Russell completed his warning. The mob looked like the Keystone Cops as they dispersed and quickly sped out of the clearing, leaving Russell, Harvey, Levi and Annie Sue alone with just the crackling of the fire to break the silence.

Annie Sue was remorseful, and it was obvious she wanted no part of Levi after this ordeal. "I just want to go home," she said. "I miss my man. Lord, just get me home."

Harvey consoled her and helped her to the police car. Levi was subdued and showed none of the bravado he exuded toward Harvey in Mae's Restaurant. "What are you going to do son?" Russell asked.

Levi responded with fear still in his voice. "I'm catching the first thing smoking out of this damn town. Think I'll go south, maybe to New Orleans. I need to get away from here. Just get me to the bus station. You won't ever see me around here again."

Later, Harvey peered from his window as he drank a cup of hot coffee and watched the sunrise. He wasn't exactly sure what happened, but he was thankful they had all lived through the harrowing night. Tommy's anxiety was relieved when Harvey and Russell brought Annie Sue home safely. He didn't even ask any questions. It was obvious she had learned a hard lesson.

As the 6:00am bus to New Orleans stopped at the depot, Harvey watched from the window of his office as Levi boarded. He saw the big bus disappear silently down the road. He had been a witness, for the first time, to the legacy of the town he now called home. This is something he would never speak to anyone about and he would never see Russell Thompson in the same light again. He would also never doubt Thompsonville was a special and powerful place.

THE GIFT
(Mary's Wish)
1979

Ragman found another half-burned cigarette butt. He struck a match and inhaled the strong and rancid tobacco deeply. He couldn't even seem to remember his real name. His memory was so fragmented, there were many things he couldn't recall. His total existence seemed to move from shelter to park bench to dark woods to grassy fields. His days were endless begging for money to buy food and wine. He had been down on his luck for a while. He didn't remember very much about his past, but what he did remember was painful. The cheap wine only seemed to give him brief relief from his pain and suffering.

Why, is the question that was constantly on his mind. Ragman was a war casualty. He was one of the living dead. Though the war he fought for his country was over, another still raged in his head. Why did he volunteer to go on patrol that day? His unit was on stand down and not scheduled to go out for another week. Their sister company was three men short and asked for volunteers. He felt a sense of duty to his country and his fellow soldiers. His mind had completely blacked out that fateful day. He only felt the pain of its memory even though the events of that horrible day were forever lost to his conscious mind.

Because of all the alcohol he drank, he no longer had "the talent". He was born with a talent for premonition. They say he, like many of the other Thompsons, inherited this talent from their ancestors. Today all he could feel was the emotions of regret and pain. His mind, it seems, was always filled with confusion. Only the cheap wine quieted the din for brief periods.

His filthy, ragged appearance was a dreadful sight. The scraggly beard had covered his face for some time. His teeth were green and rotting from lack of dental care. He had drifted from town to town for years. He had experienced brief periods of incarceration (mostly for his own protection) by local law enforcement.

Mary's time on Earth had been long. It was now the summer of 1979. She had been bedridden for one year with cancer. She was getting weaker day by day and she knew she did not have much more time. She had come to live in Thompsonville in 1925 with her daughter Gwendolyn. Leland, Gwendolyn's father and Mary's first husband, left home one day in the spring of 1920 and never returned. Mary never knew his fate. That was not unusual for the times. Black men left home looking for work many mornings and never returned. Whether they were prey to the Ku Klux

Klan, other foul play, or had just given up trying to eke out a meager living for their families is a mystery some families still ponder.

"Miss Mary," as children and adults alike of Thompsonville knew her, symbolized the spirit of the Black woman during those tough years. She and her daughter began a new life in Thompsonville. She taught for many years in the town's first formal school. She met and married Harris Thompson. They had eight children together. Annabel, Harris Jr., Anthony, Samuel, Charles, Esther, Ruth and Jimmy. Her children were a source of pride for Miss Mary. Harris was a good husband and father. When he married Mary, he accepted her daughter Gwendolyn as his own. He was the only father she remembered, and he loved her just as much as the children he and Mary had together.

"How you feel today, honey?" Harris asked as he entered her room. He had waited on her hand and foot since illness incapacitated her. He retired from the farm five years earlier.

Harris propped Mary's head up and put her breakfast tray in position next to her. He opened the curtains and the morning sun entered the room. He also replaced her candle, as was his custom each morning. It had been Mary's wish to maintain a lighted candle in her room day and night since she had become bedridden. She had said the candle would stay lit until their son Jimmy returned. Harris Thompson loved his wife dearly and indulged her wish. Though he was two years older than his wife, he still enjoyed good health. He had never been sick a day in his life. He still hunted and fished often with Samuel and their grandsons. He was also still active in the church and the community. He and his wife participated in many community activities together when she was in better health. Thompsonville had been truly blessed to have Mary and Harris Thompson.

Harris looked at the lines and tiredness around his wife's eyes. Although they had been married for forty-five years, the time had passed so quickly. He could see his dear wife's weariness and knew she hadn't slept again. Though her medication dulled the pain, it denied her restful sleep.

Each of their children had visited their sick mother over the past week (with the exception of Jimmy). "When is Jimmy coming?" she asked Harris. Harris bent his head and spoke to her softly.

"Honey, now don't start worrying about Jimmy again." The truth was, Harris nor anyone else knew where Jimmy was. Nobody knew if he was alive or dead.

Jimmy was their youngest child. When last seen, he was just a shell of the handsome, bright young man who made his parents, sisters and brothers so proud on his college graduation day.

He was a war veteran who now suffered what was termed as "battle fatigue". He returned home to Thompsonville after two tours in Viet Nam and walked the Thompsonville streets and the streets of other towns and cities for seven straight years in a dreadful state of confusion. It had been years since he was last seen or heard from. Harris secretly

hoped God had released him from his

misery. He knew his wife still prayed mightily for his safe return. He also knew the candles that burned, gave Mary comfort however, secretly he did not believe any of their family would ever see Jimmy again. Mike Jones told Harris he had seen someone who could have been Jimmy on the streets of Miami but, after a second glance, he knew he was mistaken.

Their son Anthony was now the Postmaster for the city. Charles was assistant principal at the new junior high school. Harris Jr. had been killed in action and was awarded the Silver Star Posthumously for valor. There was a time when Black men still felt a sense of duty to their country, even though their country only gave them, at best, half the rights they were entitled to as taxpaying citizens. Harris Jr.'s military service record was a source of pride for the entire family and the community of Thompsonville.

Jimmy's ordeal was worse for Mary and Harris than losing their oldest son in battle. They had now also lost their youngest son and were powerless to do anything about it. One whose life was meant to be special, was now a source of mystery, disappointment and sadness.

Not knowing a loved one's fate is a terrible ordeal. Miss Mary had endured that pain with the loss of her first husband. To endure that same pain with her youngest child, had become a severe burden.

Harris was aware of the anguish this caused his wife. As he coaxed her to swallow her pain medication, he knew it would do nothing for her real pain.

"Harris," said Mary, "I know our boy is alive. I want to see him, to talk to him once more before I go." Harris frowned. Sometimes he had to be blunt with her (which he hated to do). "Now, you hush up that kind of talk. I'm sure you'll be here longer than you think. We both know Jimmy is in God's hands wherever he is. I'm sure what happened to him was for a good reason. We've talked about this many times. You know what the VA doctor said. Most people never recover from the mental stress he suffered. I don't think there's anything we could do to help him even if he was here with us."

The expression on Miss Mary's face did not change. She had heard Harris utter those words before. Harris has been always the realist. He had always kept her grounded. "Now you get some rest. Gwendolyn and the grandchildren will be here later today."

The deathwatch had begun. Harris had called Gwendolyn a month ago to let her know her mother was getting weak and probably wouldn't last much longer. The rest of their children lived in Thompsonville.

"Hey Ragman," the children yelled. He was oblivious to the taunts and gestures offered by the youth in the neighborhood. They threw cans and rocks at him. Some hit him and some missed. He walked straight ahead with the same vacant stare. He had spent the last year here in Miami. The air was warm. He was never too cold. Tourists gave him enough money to eat and buy enough cheap wine to keep his mind numb. "Ragman" was what the kids called him. It didn't matter one way or another to him as long as he had his wine. He looked a mess. He was dirtier than ever and reeked from not having had a bath in months. He had a perpetual cough because of the drinking, smoking and poor nutrition. He was now thirty-eight, but his body was easily twenty years older.

Ragman hung around downtown with the other homeless. His fitful sleep was only broken by black unconsciousness, pain and nightmares. In his nightmares, frightening beasts always chased him. His total existence had become a nightmare from which he couldn't seem to wake up until...

Prayer is the most powerful tool God has given man. It works best when used by those who believe in its power. It is most effective when it's not selfish; that is when the fortune and welfare of someone other than the one offering that prayer is its object. Mary Thompson was a strong believer in prayer. She prayed mightily, even before she was bedridden, for the safety and welfare of all of her children including her baby boy, Jimmy. She believed her prayers had kept him safe wherever he was. Now her constant prayer was that he recover from the mental anguish that had robbed him of his youth and that he return home safely to Thompsonville.

Jimmy was her baby. He was the unexpected child. He was their "gift". She was almost forty years old when Jimmy was born. She and Harris were happy and thanked God for the unique blessing of this special life. Gwendolyn, her oldest daughter, had two children. Her oldest child was older than

Jimmy. The hope that her prayer would be answered kept Miss Mary holding on.

Ragman foraged the alleys behind the stores near downtown for food. This morning brought him to the garbage dumpster behind Ling Wu's Oriental food store. It just so happened, Ling Wu had emptied his shelves of products that were way past their shelf life earlier that morning. The contents of the dumpster provided a veritable feast for Ragman who seldom found unopened jars of anything during his garbage raids. He filled a plastic bag and meandered back to the section of the park he called his. He decided to begin his meal with a small jar labeled "Oriental Mushroom Blend". The cap on the jar was somewhat rusty and very difficult to get off, but get it off, he did. As he dug in with his fingers, he did not seem to notice the slightly rancid odor coming from the jar. The mushrooms filled his empty belly.

After eating two more jars of the mushrooms and some very stale oriental noodles, Ragman dozed off. He couldn't remember if it was the rumbling in his stomach or the pounding in his head that woke him up. Then the twitching and foaming from his mouth began. As a group of the neighborhood kids passed through the park, one remarked, "Hey look, Ragman's sick or something." They alerted one of the nearby storekeepers and the paramedics arrived in short order.

He regained consciousness in a bed, a real bed. It seemed to be a hospital. The nurse, a rotund West Indian woman, came to his bedside. She noticed he had regained consciousness.

"Well, how you feeling, Jimmy?" She spoke with a singsong

Caribbean lilt. "Welcome back to the land of the living." He thought she called him a familiar name. That name had great familiarity. *Was it his*? He felt very different today. Besides the pounding headache, his head seemed much clearer. The constant voices had quieted to small whispers. It felt as if some great darkness had finally made way for light.

He knew that, right now, all he wanted was sleep. He knew in his heart sleep would give him strength and soothe the pain he felt in his head and abdomen. He fell again into deep comforting and healing slumber.

The reflection of the face in the bedside mirror seemed old. The cheeks were hollow from poor nutrition. The eyes looked red and tired. Someone had shaved his scraggly beard. There was urgency in his gut he hadn't felt in a long time. It was quite disquieting. He needed to go home. And today he remembered where home sweet home was; Thompsonville. The last time he had a longing like this was when he first left home to go to college. "You lookin' much better today," said the nurse. "The doctor says if you had got here ten minutes later, you'd be wid the angels."

Jimmy actually smiled at her remark. He felt humor for the first time in a long time. Somehow, he knew his fortunes had changed. The events of the past weeks now seemed clearer to him than those of the past ten years. He felt as if he had awakened from a nightmare.

He only vaguely remembered the period in his life after he left Thompsonville for military service. He remembered Viet Nam and, though the pain returned, he would deal with it differently this time. Self-doubt seemed all gone now. Jimmy Thompson was starting to feel whole again.

He collected his unpaid disability monies before he left for Thompsonville. He was entitled to thirty thousand five hundred dollars in uncollected government payments for his disability. He had no intention of collecting another check for mental disability. He would use the money he received to begin reconstruction of his life. He had most of the dental work he needed completed during his stay at the hospital. He bought a nice pair of casual slacks, a flowered sport shirt and some toiletries. Ragman was no more. After additional dental care, a haircut and weeks of good food, Jimmy gained twenty pounds and was once again a handsome man. He doubted if the park kids would even recognize him. His metamorphosis was almost complete.

He boarded the bus for home the same day he was discharged from the VA Hospital. He smiled to himself when he realized the West Indian nurse had written her home telephone number inside a heart on a match cover, which she had dropped into his shirt pocket.

The hospital in Miami contacted Harris six weeks prior, when they first admitted Jimmy. He had not told Mary because he wasn't sure what to expect and he did not want her to be disappointed. His decision was now filled with doubt and regret because his dear wife had finally succumbed to her long illness this very morning Jimmy was scheduled to arrive home.

After a half hour delay, Jimmy made a change in Mobile to board the bus bound for Thompsonville. Four passengers boarded the bus in lane six which showed Jackson as its final destination.

An older Black woman was the last person to board and sat in the seat next to Jimmy. He got up to help her put her overstuffed bag into the overhead compartment. The smell of southern fried chicken emanating from her bag, brought back fond memories of his mother's Sunday meals. They exchanged greetings. She was on her way to Hattiesburg to spend some time with her daughter and her family. She was "talkative" in that sweet southern way.

As the bus passed the "Thompsonville 35 miles" sign, Jimmy had a strong premonition. He hadn't felt one of those since he was a teenager; before the war, the drugs and the alcohol. His entire family knew then, as he knew now, never to ignore his sixth sense. He had been informed earlier in the week (by hospital officials) of his mother's grave illness. He hoped to get there to see her one last time. He closed his eyes and succumbed to deep sleep.

He awoke as the bus passed the Thompsonville city limits sign. The large oak trees with long limbs and hanging moss extended across the two lane highway. They heralded Thompsonville's sleepy "way down south" look that was uniquely its own.

Jimmy felt refreshed and at peace after his brief sleep. "Mother Mary", as all her children called her, had come to him in a vision while he slept. She hugged and kissed him lovingly and whispered to him as she often did when he was a child. She had come to tell him goodbye. He still felt the comfort of her arms around him when he awoke. He knew after her sweet goodbye, her soul had passed on.

As the taxi approached the family home, it passed the Thompsonville Funeral Home hearse that carried his mother's earthly remains. As Jimmy exited the taxi, Harris, Gwendolyn and Samuel stood on the porch embracing one another in an effort to comfort themselves for their recent loss.

When Jimmy exited the taxi, his family could not believe their eyes. Harris saw his youngest son, Jimmy, appearing as handsome and healthy as ever, look towards him with recognition and expectation. He was no longer the burned out shell he remembered who always seemed to look beyond him with a vacant stare. He knew by his look and in that instant that all was now okay for "the gift" who was he and Mary's baby boy. "It's alright Daddy," Jimmy said. "Mama's real happy in her new home. She's looking down and she sees things will go well for all of us."

Harris' dear wife had departed and their lost son had returned. As one door closes, another opens. It was a touching reunion of father, son and sister and brother. They now knew Jimmy had beaten the odds. He had been delivered from the darkness of grief and misery. They walked into the house arm in arm with both tears of joy and sadness.

As Jimmy and his father entered his mother's room to allow one last chance to say an unsaid goodbye, her candle suddenly burned brightly with expectation. Though Harris was still numbed by his life mate's passing, he knew (as Jimmy had said) in his heart that she saw and was pleased with her son's return. God had indeed answered her prayer as the candle flame slowly flickered and was extinguished by the soft, gentle breeze blowing through the half open window.

THE CHARM
(1961)

Why is life so brutal? Why can't men be brothers and live in peace? The answers to these questions would do little to set young Will Thompson's heart at ease. Will was fourteen years old, five feet five inches tall and only weighed one hundred eighteen pounds, soaking wet. This was his dilemma. He was a shrimp in a world of big fish. Why do the strong always seek to inflict misery on the weak?

It was tough enough growing up Black in the south. It was even tougher when one had to defend oneself against unwarranted attacks from "overgrown bird-brained bullies".

Will looked at himself in the mirror as he did each morning while getting ready for school. He stared at a familiar and unthreatening face with peach fuzz under the chin that could not in any way be mistaken for a goatee. Some of the boys in his ninth grade class already had signs of mustaches.

He was the youngest kid in his class, as he had been since the third grade. He had been promoted from second grade to third grade after only three weeks because he was able to do the work and was way ahead of the other students in his class. The school work in third grade was more challenging, but he had always considered being moved ahead a class a curse, because he was always one of the smaller boys in his class.

He was now in the tenth grade. Today he regretted having to go to his second period class because he sat next to Dub Jones during that hour.

"Hey Thompson, meet me behind the gym at three o'clock and we're going to settle this thing between you and me," Dub whispered to him in a menacing tone.

What thing? Will thought. Dub was six feet one, two hundred pounds of muscle and meanness and he was the class bully.

The thing to be settled, of course, was Rosita Anderson. Rosita was the prettiest girl and the star pupil of Will's ninth grade class. Dub liked Rosita very much. Will also liked Rosita. She was not only pretty, but easily the nicest girl in his class. Though Rosita insisted Dub was not her boyfriend, nobody challenged Dub's claim that she was his girl and his alone. Dub was jealous to the extent that he had broken Lonnie Jones' nose in a "one punch" fight last week because he heard Lonnie was going to ask Rosita to the spring dance for freshmen.

Will was afraid. This guy's size alone was a weapon against him. He could fall on him and hurt him. Dub was not pleased when he found out Will and Rosita sat together during lunch in the cafeteria the previous day.

"I heard you was eating lunch with my girlfriend, Rosita yesterday," he snorted at Will.

"I didn't know she was your girlfriend," Will casually replied. This was an idiotic thing to say to an already *irate idiot*.

"Thompson I should kill you now for talking big like that," he barked, and if the last bell for the fifth period hadn't just rang, he may have done just that right there in the classroom.

Sammy and Johnny Parker, Will's friends praised him for standing up to Dub. It was a darn good thing they couldn't feel the terror in his heart.

As Will sat through his sixth period class, his mind came back from never-never land when Ms. Wheaton asked him, "Mr. Thompson, when did the American Civil War begin?"

He was awakened from his reverie by her question. "Excuse me, Ms. Wheaton, could you repeat the question?" he asked.

There was a soft chuckle from the class as it was apparent to all he had been distracted and was now buying time until he could collect his wits. Momentarily, he then proceeded to give a correct response to her question. "The Civil War began in 1861 when shots were fired on Fort Sumter."

The issue with Dub Jones had become a real problem. It was ten past two and Will had no clue as to how he would save his bacon or at least prevent it from being burnt to a crisp. But wait, maybe there was something. This was really a stretch, but he remembered the charm his Cousin Russell had given him when he was ten years old.

Cousin Russell was Will's hero. Russell was a much older cousin on his father's side. He was very intelligent and well-traveled for a Black man during those times. Russell was only two years younger than Will's father Newton. He was, by profession, a horse trainer who spent the summer months in Kentucky and the fall and winter in Thompsonville. He was not a bad looking man, according to the gossip from the neighborhood ladies. He did not project the air of most Black men of his time. He was well-spoken and those who did not know, could have easily mistaken him for a doctor, school principal or a college professor. There was so much more to Russell and Will could easily discern how special he was.

When Russell was in Thompsonville, he lived with Will and his family. Momma said Cousin Russell's family was all deceased and Daddy was the closest family he had left in Thompsonville. It was quite a tragedy years ago when Russell's wife and children were lost in a fire on their farm. He lost his wife, his mother and all six of his young sons in a fire on the coldest December night the town had ever known.

Russell and Will's father, Newton had always been close. Will's parents had taken him in and helped him to get over that terrible event of his life. His mother confided that that

Cousin Russell was a changed man and was very different from the person he was before the fire.

When Cousin Russell was home, there was much excitement in their house. People stopped by to see him constantly. The phone rang for him continuously. Most of the people who came to the house seemed desperate or agitated when they came in. They would go to the guest room with Cousin Russell and he would close the door. The people seemed at peace or in good spirits when they left out. Will didn't understand the significance of this, at the time. He knew this could only mean Russell had done something to cause this change. Besides, his father, Newton was a Deacon in the church. Newton liked Cousin Russell as much as Will did and Russell would never betray his trust.

One night after supper when all the folks had come and gone, Will and Cousin Russell sat alone on the front porch gazing at the star filled sky. They talked of many things. Cousin Russell had that special way of making everybody in his presence feel at ease and important.

Russell spoke to him, "Will, you know there are many things to be thankful for. Every person on Earth has worth. Each of us has unique gifts given to us by the Creator. It's up to each of us to recognize these gifts and share them with our fellow man. Our gifts may be in any area; science, the arts, sports, or just the ability to ease the pain and suffering others feel in everyday living. I know you will find your gift and give back freely to humanity as I have tried to do. You should also know that there is both good and evil in the world. Evil, can befall even the most righteous person. Here's something I want you to have."

Russell placed an object in Will's hand. It was a metal disc the size of a silver dollar. It was very worn from age. The disc was heavier than it looked. One could only guess how old it was. The object had a figure etched into the shape of a tribal warrior. It had a magical and unique appearance that appealed to Wil. "This belonged to our great ancestor who lived her life and died a slave on a plantation in Georgia. Hold onto it. Keep it close to you at all times and no evil will ever befall you. This I guarantee." Will looked closely at the charm. It gave off an energy that made him feel warm inside.

The significance of what his cousin said did not totally sink in. Will was basically a good kid who was never in any real trouble and always tried to live (as his mother said) by the good book. He had, however, since that night, always carried the charm with him in his right pocket.

It was 2:40pm when Will heard Billy Simpson bet Carl Brown that there would be only two blows passed in the fight. Dub would hit Will and he would hit the ground. Marvin Welk insisted there would be no fight because, "That sissy Will Thompson would probably be too afraid to come out of the building." Will could only listen to this derogatory banter without responding.

He would show up. As afraid as he was, not showing up was not an option. His Dad and Cousin Russell had both told him on separate occasions, in different words, he must stand up to life's challenges, even when the odds seemed insurmountable. He had been in fights before. What child in Mississippi hadn't by his age? He had never been in one where the odds seemed this stacked against him. His previous altercations had been nothing more than minor scuffles. Those were also against kids his size.

Will was very good at talking his way out of situations, but he witnessed the fight between Lonnie Jones and Dub. Dub would hear no discussion from Lonnie. Dub was brutal. He was a hard case who resented those he termed "smart boys" like Will. In truth, he was always looking for any excuse to pummel anybody half his size.

It was now 2:50pm. Will had to catch his bus at the very spot Dub had chosen for their showdown. There would be a large audience to witness his very public execution. Will took the charm from his pocket and held it tightly in his left hand.

As he recalled, nothing bad had befallen him since Uncle Russell gave this to him. In spite of his dilemma, there was something comforting about holding the charm. It was 2:59pm and Ms. Wheaton was giving out homework assignments. Will was so preoccupied with his personal predicament, he didn't even bother to write the assignments down.

As the bell rang promptly at 3:00pm, he gathered his belongings and started the long walk to the bus stop. It was as if he had the plague. Even his close friends left him to walk alone in his darkest hour.

As he walked by, people would stop talking and look the other way. When Will passed through the double doors to the outside of the building, he had his text books in his right hand and the charm firmly grasped in his left hand. He was not certain at first, but now he was sure it was throbbing in his hand. It had a warm, comforting sensation that seemed to penetrate his entire being. He was glad to know Rosita would not be there to see what could possibly be his demise. She did not ride the bus. Her family was one of the few Black families who owned an automobile and her mother was always there to pick her up each day when school was out.

He opened his hand to look at the charm as he continued his walk. It was not physically different, but it seemed to give off a warmth that he could definitely feel. His fear was eased in that moment. He then remembered the people who came to see Russell and how at ease they appeared when they left. He didn't know how, but he knew he would be pulled through this predicament.

As Will arrived at his bus stop, the crowd had already formed. He could hear "Let's get this show on the road." "Tear his head off Dub." Will thought, *People were really barbaric when someone else was doing the fighting*. This crowd was ready to see blood spilled.

Dub was standing in the middle of the crowd. He had taken off his shirt showing off his muscles. He began shadow boxing when Will arrived. The gold tooth in his mouth glistened along with the sheen of his *homemade process hairdo* in the afternoon sun.

The crowd parted like the Red Sea when Dub walked toward Will with a menacing scowl, and said, "All right Thompson, prepare to meet your maker." He pounded his closed fist into his open hand as he gave Will a frightening and intimidating stare.

Will, who was much smaller than Dub as they stood face to face, only smiled and said," Dub, let's talk about this. I'm sure we can settle it another way." It was indeed a lame thing to say, but it was all the sound that came from his mouth.

"We don't have anything to talk about" snarled Dub. The crowd cheered. They would get the fight, they wanted. And with that comment, things began to happen. Bizarre things. Will peered into the crowd to see his friends, Sammy and Johnny. Their faces mirrored absolute terror.

At that exact moment, Dub wound up to throw a Haymaker and Will felt the charm pulsing wildly in his hand as his mind almost went completely blank. It was if someone else was now in control of him. As Dub's big fist whistled at warp speed past his chin, Will could feel the bad intent in the breeze created by Dub's intended blow. His head involuntarily moved just the inch and a half necessary to avoid being destroyed by the tremendous punch. The crowd gave a huge sigh as he missed. What happened next was just as improbable and funny. Dub tripped awkwardly over Will's left foot because he was so committed to landing his big blow. He went flying, face first, into the dust and gravel. The crowd laughed with ferocity as Dub righted himself. He had dust all over his body, his face and in his processed hairdo. He was a horrible sight. He looked like a "dusty ghost", as Sammy Parker would later describe him. He was greatly embarrassed by the crowd's laughter and in some pain from his ungraceful fall.

"All right sissy, fight like a man," Dub snarled as he charged at Will again. Will was only a fair athlete and not much of a fighter, but on this day and at this time he made the right moves at the right time. He stood his ground as Dub again charged him. Will made a swift Matador's move to his left and his right foot extended just enough in Dub's path to trip him and again send him flying. This time he was really airborne. He slid on his belly, head first for about eighteen feet into the front right wheel of Washington County School bus number 66613. His head made a dull "thud" as it contacted the hard rubber of the school bus' tire. He was in serious pain now as he tried to right himself again. The gravel had created numerous cuts and abrasions on his chest and arms.

Dub had a strange perplexed look on his face as he struggled to get to his feet with blood oozing from his cuts. Will was absolutely sure those were big goose tears in his eyes. Dub Jones AKA *the class bully* was now looking for a way out of this.

"Hey, Thompson, take it easy on him!" someone in the crowd yelled.

"Looks like you finally met your match Dub!" someone else yelled.

"He's not so tough now!" yet another voice said.

Two male physical education teachers, who had heard the commotion, came outside and began to disperse the crowd.

This was a real short fight and Dub was already finished. He was glad it was over. Dub was taken to the Principal's office to have his wounds treated and dressed. Will was not even approached by the teachers. Who would have believed he (Will) could have inflicted that much damage to Dub Jones? Dub certainly wasn't going to voluntarily admit Will Thompson had bested him, but everyone who was there knew the truth.

As Will boarded his bus the students cheered, "Way to go Will!"

"Yeah you showed him!"

"It's about time that jerk got what he deserved!"

Will rode home in a seat by himself. He clung to his charm as he exited the bus and walked the rest of the way home. He and everyone else knew they wouldn't have to worry about Dub's harassment again.

Life is a constant struggle between good and evil. Some days evil wins and some days good wins. In the cosmic conclusion, good will always eventually triumph, and on this day, in a battle against the odds, good indeed triumphed (of course with a little help).

SEVENTH SON
(Evil Roy)
(1966)

Southern backwoods towns off the beaten path were not safe places for Negroes to travel in the 1960s. Brewton, a small town in southeast Mississippi, was such a town. A weather worn statue of a Confederate soldier, with rifle in hand, stood in Brewton Park in the center of town. The inscription etched into its base read, *Read Nigger and Run. If you can't read, run anyway.* This was a source of humor and pride for some residents of Brewton.

Though Brewton was an all White town, younger and smarter businessmen realized this inscription was an eyesore which intimidated outside Whites and Coloreds alike and prevented both from spending much time or money in their town. The young businessmen didn't care for the Yankees or Niggers either, but their money was as good as anyone else's.

Many of the community businesses in town barely made

expenses. Roy Wiggins was the Deputy Chief. His father, Sam Wiggins, was the Brewton Chief of Police. Roy was a chip off the old block. He was just as mean as his dad; probably meaner. Sam Wiggins also served as the Grand Dragon of the area Ku Klux Klan. Sam often bragged, when he got drunk about how many Niggers the Brewton area Klan had lynched. The truth was, the Klan's days were numbered in Brewton and the south.

The main thoroughfare through Brewton was Mississippi Highway 27. Further down the road about ten miles, was Thompsonville. Thompsonville was Brewton's polar opposite. Its population was all Black.

The local hangout in Brewton was The Rebel Yell, (a Honky Tonk on Highway 27 on the outskirts of town). When Roy Wiggins wasn't setting speed traps for the Yankees, or unsuspecting Coloreds who were lost, his police cruiser was usually parked outside the Rebel Yell.

It was Saturday night in Brewton. The parking lot was full. Inside the club, Ray Parker was drunk, as usual, telling Coon jokes. He had a million of them and when he was drunk he tried to tell them all. "What are two things you can't give a Nigger?" He asked loudly. Before anyone could reply, he yelled loudly, "A black eye and a job."

The crowd around the bar roared. All these fools wanted to do was laugh at Nigger jokes, thought Roy. "When is somebody gonna lynch a Coon instead of jus' telling jokes about 'em?" Roy asked in a serious tone to nobody in particular.

Roy Wiggins was a large well-built man with a hair trigger

temper. Though he was the deputy chief, he was the kind of man who made even decent White folks feel nervous seeing a gun on his hip.

"Take it easy Roy," Lonnie Jones said. "We hung so many Niggers around here about ten years ago we probably scared 'em all off. Besides the FBI up Jackson way is starting to crack down on Klan activities. You know that. "

"What are they going to do?" Roy asked. "Arrest good White citizens for hanging a bunch of porch monkeys?"

"Times are changing Roy, you know that," replied Ray. "Even the good White businessmen here in Brewton are startin' to sing a different tune."

"I'll believe that when I see it", said Roy.

"Say, there's plenty ah Niggahs over in Thompsonville. I know we can find a couple over there to string up," Roy remarked.

At that comment, Sam Wiggins, his father who had been quietly listening made a comment. His demeanor was suddenly serious, "You know Thompsonville is off limits. We don't bother the Blacks over there," said Sam.

"And what's so damn special about dem?" Roy questioned.

This road had been already trod. Sam had always insisted none of the Blacks in Thompsonville be harassed by the Klan. Some of the younger Klan members felt like Roy but none would challenge the word of Sam Wiggins. He was a Grand Dragon, mostly because he was the most feared. No man in Brewton questioned his motives.

The beer was starting to go to Roy's head. He had lost control of his tongue. His next comment was directed toward his father. "I guess you must be turning into a Niggah love..." Roy was six feet, two inches tall and about two hundred and forty pounds and twenty-two years older than his only son. Roy never quite got the "r" out of his mouth at the end of the word "lover". Sam slapped Roy so hard it sounded as if a gunshot had gone off inside the Rebel Yell.

The club became deathly quiet. Everyone knew Roy had stepped across the line. "Dammit, as long as you draw breath on the face of this Earth, don't you ever call me that," Sam said. Roy stood there as tears welled up in his large blue eyes. He knew better than to challenge his father in public or private. He had a pained look on his reddened face as he stormed from the Rebel Yell.

Roy patrolled the streets of Brewton in an effort to calm himself down. He made his entire patrol route and again came up Highway 27 towards the Rebel Yell. He passed an old beat up Ford pickup travelling the opposite direction towards Thompsonville. Three Negroes were in the cab of the pickup. He observed that the truck had a rear tail light out and promptly made a U- turn and turned on his flashers.

Newton Thompson came into Mae's Diner about 7:45pm. He had walked the two miles from his farm into town. Newton grew a lot of the vegetables and raised most of the pork for Thompsonville on his forty acre farm just outside town. He had nine children, the last seven of them sons who helped him operate the farm. They worked the farm hard, six days a week He had let his boys off early this day to have some time for themselves.

Arthur, Charles and his youngest son Will had left about one thirty to go hunting over in Summerland. It was only about ten miles from Thompsonville but that was if one drove through Brewton. Newt nor any other Blacks in Thompsonville drove through Brewton to go to Summerland or anywhere else. They would take Highway 16 to Highway 22, and back to Highway 27. This detour was about five miles out of the way. Newt had told the boys to be home by sundown. Newton's sons were his pride and joy. He had never had any trouble with any of them disobeying him.

This was the winter season and the sun had set at 5:30pm. At 7:00pm, after they had not returned or called, Newt began his walk to town. "Anybody seen my sons, Arthur, Charles and William?" he asked, speaking loudly to no particular person in the diner.

Eddie Thompson, his distant cousin, who was a fixture at Mae's Diner responded, "Not me. Where'd they go Newt?" "They left in the pickup to do some hunting over in Summerland. They were supposed to be home by dark. It's not like my boys to disobey me."

"My goodness," said Mae from behind the counter. "You

walked all the way from the farm in that cold. Here's some hot coffee to warm you up."

Carl Johnson, another distant cousin asked Newt, "You reckon they went thru Brewton? I know you save fifteen minutes goin' that way, but it's dangerous for us Coloreds to pass through that hole anytime."

"My boys are smart enough not to do that," said Newt.

The truth was, on this night they weren't. They were late and Arthur, who was the oldest and the driver, had been persuaded by Charles to go through Brewton to save time and get home shortly after sundown. That would insure their Daddy wouldn't be as mad.

Summerland was nothing more than a minor ripple in the highway. It only had a country store and a filling station. The Peterson family sold goods to the Coloreds and allowed Newton Thompson and his boys to hunt on the acreage they owned behind their store. The Petersons were decent Whites for these times in Mississippi. Negroes did not have to enter the back door to purchase goods in their store, however, if other Whites were in the store, they had to show respect by allowing those Whites to be waited on whether they were there first or not. It was a concession most Thompsonville Negroes accepted since Summerland was closer and saved them the forty-mile trip to Hattiesburg.

The boys had chased a large buck most of the afternoon. Daddy would be excited when they brought deer meat home. They had cornered the deer about five o'clock. Charles and Art both got off good shots and brought him down. They were excited about bagging the deer. Art was nineteen years old, Charles was eighteen and Will the youngest was sixteen.

Will did not hunt. He only tagged along to *take care of* Art and Charlie. By the time the boys carried the big buck to the truck and got him loaded up, it was already 5:30pm.

"We're late already," Charlie said to Art. "We could save twenty minutes by going through Brewton."

"Daddy told us never to do that, "responded Will.

"It's Saturday night," said Charlie. "Dem Peckerwoods are probly getting all liquored up at that redneck Honky Tonk. They won't even know we passed thu, and you better not tell Papa," he said as he gave Will a menacing look.

Art and Charlie both loved "Baby Bro" as Will was called by the family. All of that mumbo jumbo about the seventh son of a seventh son certainly applied to him. He wouldn't kill anything and didn't even eat meat. He was different from the other boys in the family. He was the youngest and the smallest in the statue of the boys thus Mama had always been protective of him, but young William always pulled his share of the load around the farm. He spent most of his free time with Cousin Russell under the big oak tree by the lake. Because he was his father's seventh son, Cousin Russell said that made him special.

Roy Wiggins could hardly control his enthusiasm as he got out of the cruiser and walked up to the beat-up '48 Ford pickup. He drew his pistol and approached the cab. He had a flashlight in one hand and his cocked revolver in the other. He wasn't afraid of any Nigger, but you never knew.

"All right, you Niggers, out of the truck with your hands up," he said loudly.

As all three exited the truck with frightened looks on their faces, Roy was only slightly disappointed that they were only teenage boys. They would still suit his purpose. Hate ran deep in this man's heart. Sympathy for anyone Black was an emotion Roy Wiggins had never felt.

"Lemme see your driver's license and registration Nigger," he barked at Art. With a shaking outstretched hand Art produced both items. Because of his nervousness and anxiety, Art accidently dropped the registration card on the ground. This startled Roy Wiggins. Suddenly and without warning, Roy hit Art as hard as he could with the heavy-duty flashlight. The blow struck Art with a sickening thud to his right temple. With blood spurting on Charlie and Will, Art's lifeless body crumpled to the ground beside the truck.

Charlie screamed in terror and bent down to help Art who lay prone on the cold ground. "Niggah, if you touch him I'll blow your brains out," sneered Roy with his cocked revolver pointed just three inches from Charlie's head.

The blow was hard enough to kill. Because of the way Arthur had fallen, and because he was deathly still and not breathing, both boys knew this evil White man had senselessly murdered their brother.

Meanwhile, back at Mae's Diner, the folks gathered were trying to figure out how and where to start looking for the boys. "Newt, I'll tell you, we should get our guns and go over to Brewton to look for dem boys," Carl Johnson said.

"And what are you going to do when you get there?" Mae said. "This is still Mississippi and this is 1966. A colored man's life ain't worth a whole lot in this country. You men need a better idea." They all agreed. All Negroes in Thompsonville knew to steer a wide berth around Brewton.

Emmit Smith volunteered to let Newt and Carl use his truck to retrace the boys' route to Summerland. They probably had a flat or maybe the truck broke down. This sounded like a good idea and everyone agreed it was probably the most practical thing to do.

As Newt and Carl got up to leave, the diner door slowly opened and in walked Russell Thompson. He was all of fifty years old, but he was still very spry with salt and pepper hair. He was also Newton's second cousin, although they were more like brothers. His patronage at Mae's Diner this time of night was also a surprise. Russell was an icon in the Thompsonville community. His grandparents were ex-slaves who were part of the original group who moved to Mississippi from Georgia before the turn of the century.

All of Thompsonville believed Russell had the gift of foresight. He never gave bad advice and it was said that it was he who was responsible for most of the town's prosperity.

He was a mild-mannered man who never spoke loud, but the tone and pitch of his voice commanded attention. "Now just wait a minute," he said to Newt and Carl. Even if your boys ran into a little trouble in Brewton, everything will be okay," he said to Newt. Newt was only two years his senior, but respected his position in this town.

"But how do you know that?" questioned Eddie with a look of grave doubt on his face. There was that small percentage of non-believers.

"Eddie, don't be a fool all of your life," said Mae. "Just shut up and listen to what Mr. Russell says."

"I thought that the Chief of Police promised he would never bother anybody from Thompsonville," said Emmit to Russell.

"He did and he's kept his promise, but some others have made no such promise."

Just then, Ezra Jones, the town undertaker, entered the diner. He had a mournful look on his face and held his hat in both hands as he spoke softly to Newt.

"I just got a call from the Brewton Police to come over and pick up the body of a Thompsonville boy, Arthur Abel Thompson, who was killed resisting arrest by the Brewton police."

Everyone but Russell Thompson was standing there with shocked looks on their faces. This moment was the true test of Thompsonville's faith in its prophet. Russell Thompson had helped make this town. His stubbornness, prodding and urging had helped create the oasis of Thompsonville. Eddie had once before questioned his judgment. He would have to be very careful about what he said at this second. In spite of this shocking revelation, he sensed his young protégé, William, was still somehow in control of the situation.

"Have I led you wrong before?" he asked. Nobody responded, but there were looks of great distress and sadness in the room. Twenty black and brown faces were all deathly quiet.

"I'm sure there's been a mistake made Ezra... You can make the trip over to Brewton but I believe you'll be doing it for nothing and it's dangerous over there for any Black man, even one in your profession."

"Newt, it's about time I remind you and the whole town of this fact. Your son Will, is a seventh son. We in Thompsonville have managed to survive by the tradition passed us by our slave mother, Dora Jane. I have my birthright, which you all know about. You have also seen the tradition of Dora Jane demonstrated in many others of us, but Will is the chosen one. I have seen the signs. In him, there will be no doubt. Now I ask all of you to stay put. By 9:30pm all three of those boys will come through that door safe and sound."

Russell saw no such thing. He had told a necessary lie to prevent another possible tragedy. He just had a feeling Will would bring them through whatever problem they had encountered. At last, it was on the table. Now, maybe Newton and the rest of the family would start to see young

William in a new light. Russell had faith that all of the gifts of the Thompson clan would one day be manifested through his younger cousin.

Will and Charlie sat handcuffed in the back of the police cruiser. Roy called over the two-way radio to ask the dispatcher to contact the Negro funeral home in Thompsonville to have the meat wagon pick up a *Nigra youth* who was killed resisting arrest in Brewton - one "Arthur Abel Thompson." The term *Nigra* was as close as Roy Wiggins ever got to using a non-derogatory term for Blacks. He then went into his trunk to get a tarp to cover the body.

Charlie was sobbing softly when William took control of the situation. He folded his hands over once and his handcuffs dropped to the vehicle floor with a clang. As Charlie witnessed this, he immediately stopped crying. Will then placed both hands on Charlie's face and wet them in the tears which streamed down his older brother's face. Charlie was amazed by Will's actions. "Will, how did you do that," he whispered. Will did not answer and turned and bumped the locked door of the police car ever so slightly. It opened without a sound.

He then got out and began to walk toward Roy, who was kneeling over Art's inert body. By the time Roy realized the Black youth was free and upon him, it was too late. As he turned and faced Will with a look of alarm on his face, Will gently touched him with his right index finger right between his eyes. The left index finger went deep into Roy's solar plexus. His touch incapacitated Roy and left him frozen with a vacant stare in his eyes.

Will walked around him, as if he were a lifeless statue, and then removed the tarp from Art's lifeless body. He was lying in a pool of blood left by the severe head wound he suffered at the hand of Roy Wiggins. Art's soul had departed. His eyes stared fixedly into nowhere, his skin was cold to the touch and no breath was in his body.

A tear rolled down Will's left cheek He wiped it with his right hand. He then bent over and put both index fingers into the open wound on Art's right temple. He applied gentle pressure for about three minutes. He then rose and took the handcuff key from Roy's belt and walked back to the cruiser. Roy was still immobile, staring off into space with a surprised look on his face with one hand on his still holstered revolver.

Will opened the door and looked Charlie in the face. Charlie's face held a look of pure terror. "Will, our brother is dead and we're gonna get the lectric chair for sure if the Klan don't lynch us first," moaned Charlie.

Will shook him to get his attention. "Charlie, listen to me," "When I take off your cuffs, go and get into the truck and you are going to start driving Art and me to Thompsonville; we won't stop until we get to Mae's Diner on Front Street. Is that clear?"

Charlie was still very upset as he stumbled out of the cruiser and walked quickly toward the truck. Will retrieved Art's license and vehicle registration from the front seat of the cruiser. He then keyed into the two-way radio and spoke in a voice which sounded exactly like Roy Wiggins, "Emmy-Lou, this is Roy."

"Go ahead Roy," she said.

"Have you entered my last communication into the log?" he asked.

"Not yet. I'm on my break. I did call the colored funeral home in Thompsonville, and they said they would send a hearse," she responded.

"Emmy-Lou, what is your full name"?

"Why Emmy Lou Bowers," she answered.

"And what is your favorite dessert?" he asked again. "Apple," she replied. Emmy Lou had a crush on Roy and she more than welcomed a social conversation with him.

Will could still hear Emmy-Lou's voice as he walked toward the truck, "Why, Emmy Lou Bowers." "Apple Pie." "Why Emmy-Lou Bowers." "Apple Pie." "Why Emmy-Lou Bowers," "Apple Pie,".... She was stuck!

When Will returned, Art was now starting to stir. Will went over and helped him walk groggily to the truck. Charlie slowly drove the truck back onto the highway. Art was slumped in the middle and Will sat next to the passenger window. Roy was still kneeling by the road at the spot where the truck had stopped. He was still sporting a vacant look on his face. His left hand was on his holstered revolver as Emmy-Lou's voice droned on and on the two-way radio.

"Will, I know Art was dead. What did you do? There's not even a mark on his head where that crazy Peckerwood hit him. And look at all of that blood still on his coat," Charlie said in an agitated voice.

Through this experience, William Thompson had become a man in his brother's eyes. During this difficult situation, his attitude and demeanor toward his older brother had changed. "Charlie, we still have two more blocks before we're out of Brewton. Now shut up, pay attention and get us back home."

They made the drive safely back to Thompsonville. Art slept all the way back. He awoke as the truck passed the Thompsonville City limits sign. "Boy, I must a really been tired," he said. "What time is it?"

"9:45," responded Will.

"I hope Papa's so glad to get this deer meat, he decides not to kill us all," said Art. Both Will and Charlie reacted slightly to Art's choice of words.

"Art, I'm sure Papa's worried sick about us, let's stop by Mae's Diner to see if he's there," said Will.

Mae normally closed the diner at nine but as the boys pulled up, the lights were still on. Emmit Smith's truck and Ezra's hearse were both parked outside.

Russell's bluff had been called. Eddie Thompson had started his swagger. "Well, Russell, its nine forty seven and dem boys ain't..." Before Eddie could finish his sentence all three Thompson boys walked into the Diner. A mass sigh of astonishment and relief was audible from those who still remained.

"Where you boys been?" Newt asked. The entire diner was waiting for their answer. Charlie attempted to respond.

"Well Papa, we was tryin to catch this big buck. We must have chased him all over them Summerland woods. We caught..."

Newt interrupted him. "What happened in Brewton?"

William began, "We were late and trying to get home as soon as we could. Our only chance was to go through Brewton. A policeman stopped us and........"

At that point Russell interjected. "It's getting late. We're all relieved you boys are okay. I'm going home." With that comment he exited the front door.

"Where did all of that blood on your jacket come from?" Mae asked Art. Art observed and gave a puzzled look. "We caught this big Buck. Art and I carried toted him a long ways out of dem woods. It must be from that," Charlie answered.

He gave a brief but pained look in Will's direction. "Papa," Charlie continued, "there's a lot of deer meat out in the truck. We all tired and hungry. Would like to git that deer dressed before turning in tonight."

That sounded like a good idea. Newton was relieved that his sons were okay, but was now concerned they may be afoul of the law in Brewton. "You boys in any trouble with the law in Brewton?"

"What Law?" commented Carl, "You mean dem Klan wit badges?"

Everyone knew many unsuspecting Negroes had met their doom after being stopped by Brewton Police.

At that moment, Newton Thompson looked into the faces of all three boys, but sought an answer from Arthur, the eldest. The response came from the least expected source, William. "Papa, we had a minor problem over there. We didn't harm anyone. Nobody is looking for us. We wouldn't do anything to bring shame to our family or our town. Have faith in me when I tell you everything is okay."

It was then Newt saw his youngest son assert himself. He began to see him in a different light. Southern Negro men were valued during those times on how much physical strength they had and how much work they could do to help their family survive. The confidence in Will's voice gave comfort not only to Newton but all of the anxious faces in Mae's Diner. This was the same child who would not kill or even clean the animals Newt and his other sons hunted. There was indeed something unique and special about him like Cousin Russell had said. At that very moment, Newt saw and appreciated it. And so did Art and Charlie. "Come on," said Newt. Let's get home. Your Mama's worried."

MAGIC SEASON
(1964)

Before the Los Angeles Lakers or the Boston Celtics of the 1970s or the Philadelphia 76ers or the mighty Chicago Bulls, was the Thompsonville Blue Hornets. The Blue Hornets were renowned for their prowess in football, which has always been king in Mississippi.

1963 was a unique season for the Thompsonville basketball Fighting Blue Hornets. Never before had Mississippi sports seen a feat as was performed by the Blue Hornets that season.

The basketball team for Thompsonville High had never even won half of their games in a season. Never had basketball captivated the attention of the town and the surrounding communities as it did during this special season. Thompsonville High School had fifteen state football championship trophies, six runners up and fifteen track and field state championship trophies for men and sixteen for women. They had no championships, at all, for basketball.

Thompsonville High had floored its first basketball team

two seasons after it fielded football and track teams in the Negro Big 10 Athletic Conference. This was the premier sports organization for Negro high school athletic competition in the state since 1936. Thompsonville had held its own and, in some stretches, dominated the competition during its participation.

They had recently opened its new gymnasium, which seated twenty five hundred. This was almost half the population of the town. The school board had some dissension about constructing such a large facility when basketball was such a small sport. The fact that the town's population was only sixty three hundred was not a valid argument against the gymnasium, since the football stadium seated five thousand.

Pop Thompson, the basketball coach, had pleaded a good case for its construction. "Basketball," he insisted, "would become a much bigger sport in the seventies and eighties and on through the turn of the century. It has the potential to be more entertaining than football and if more money were put into facilities and training, Thompsonville would have more competitive men and women's teams. Thompsonville High School (THS) could then place even more students on college athletic scholarship."

Pop Thompson had been coaching since the program began in 1938. He was now sixty two years old and had not known a winning season before this one. The 1955 team had come close but failed miserably in the regional finals championship game against Brooks High School of Jackson.

The old gymnasium, which seated eight hundred, had standing room only for that game. This 1963-64 season would be Pop's last coaching season for Thompsonville High. He had won the battle with the school board regarding the new gymnasium, but only on the condition that Pop step down as coach after its first year of use. The board would recruit a new coach after this season.

It was Charlie Ford's opinion that the game had passed Pop by long ago and that new blood may be able to take Thompsonville youth to that future Pop had predicted for basketball.

Of course, Pop had agreed. His major concern was for his players. Though he had never had a championship team, all of Pop's former players were successful people. His major concern had always been his young men.

Pop, in addition to being the men's basketball coach, was an accomplished chemistry teacher at Thompsonville High. He took pride in the high scores Thompsonville students made in the chemistry part of the College Board tests. He also inspired his players to value education, even above their athletic ability. During these times, big money in professional sports was not yet a reality for athletes in America. It was not even a pipe dream for the Black athlete.

It was the first Saturday in March 1964. The stage was set to play the championship game for the state Negro Big 10 Basketball crown in the Thompsonville High School Gymnasium at 8:00pm. The Fighting Blue Hornets were the talk of the state in both the Negro and White sports press.

For the first time ever, Thompsonville High had that winning season, breaking their personal won-loss best by a wide margin.

They were twenty and one during the regular season with three straight wins in the playoffs. Pop Thompson was now a local celebrity. He couldn't go anywhere without receiving advice from those he came in contact with. Specifically, advice was offered on how to win the championship game.

The atmosphere was exciting for his 1955 team, but this was something very different. The whole town was electric. Though the Blue Hornets had won the state football championship this year, the excitement over their basketball season was something really special.

This was new territory for Pop and the town. He had a sour look on his face as he entered Mae's Diner. "Hi Pop," yelled Eddie Thompson from his seat at the luncheon counter. "Are the Fighting Blue Hornets ready for Brooks High?"

Pop always figured Eddie to be a strange sort, even for Thompsonville. The Brooks High School Jaguars seemed to be the perennial nemesis of Thompsonville athletics and Pop Thompson. Sherlock Holmes had Moriarty. Custer had Sitting Bull. The Thompsonville Fighting Blue Hornets had the Brooks High School Jaguars. It seemed as if Brooks relished its role as spoiler. Brooks gave the team of '55 the loss which guaranteed another losing season for Thompsonville basketball and ruined their chance to advance to the state finals. This 1963 team was the first championship team in Thompsonville High history. The only regular season loss this season was to Brooks High. The Jackson Press had made Brooks strong favorites to break the hearts of the best basketball team Thompsonville High had ever floored.

"As ready as they will ever be," Pop responded. Eddie Thompson was one of the main members of the school board calling for Pop's head when the hearing for the new gymnasium was held. Now that the team was winning, Eddie greeted Pop as if they were long lost friends. Pop did not take any of the *politics* personal. He was going to retire from coaching no matter what the outcome of tonight's game. He had fought the good fight. It was now time to give in to younger blood and move on to something else.

"What'll it be Pop?" asked Mae.

"Let me have the special," he answered. The lunch special was fried chicken, collard greens, cornbread, black-eyed peas, sweet potato pie and a large glass of sweet lemon tea. It was a good value at $1.25 which included the teacher's discount. Mae's Diner was still the most popular place to eat in Thompsonville in the early 1960s.

Pop had spent the morning in his office reviewing the strategy for his team against Brooks High. This team was already the most successful in Thompsonville's history, but his legacy as a basketball coach would be summed up tonight. That was the source of his consternation.

This team had bested good teams which included those from Brookhaven, Yazoo City and McComb. The biggest game the Blue Hornets won this season was against Gulfport

Northshore in overtime by one point. Their one loss was to Brooks in a non-division game by ten big points in Jackson. The larger schools were difficult opposition for schools like Thompsonville High.

Pop's team didn't have size, but they were fast, intelligent, intense and most of all, they had heart. They believed in their coach. Sean Johnson was the only senior on the team. Sean had lost his family in a car accident last winter on Highway 27. Since he had no other relatives in town, Pop had taken him in. People in Thompsonville always found a way to take care of the community's orphaned children when tragedy struck.

Sean's Aunt Dealy in Detroit had agreed to let him live with Pop until he graduated High School. Sean was a good student, but his prospects for getting an academic scholarship were not nearly as good as those for getting a basketball scholarship. Pop and his wife Angela never had children so they enjoyed having Sean, although they were unprepared to assist him financially with college. All of these worries made Pop's stomach churn as he sat at the lunch counter.

"Is Sean up for a scholarship to play at State?" Eddie asked.

"Coach Wilson hasn't shown any interest in him. I think he's looking for more height for his last two scholarship slots," answered Pop. "I have talked to Coach Wiley at Southern in Louisiana. He'll be at the game scouting Sean tonight."

"Sean's such a nice kid," said Mae. "I hope things work out

for him."

Pop finished his meal and began his walk back to his office in the new gymnasium. As he crossed First Street, he saw a familiar figure approaching. It was his distant Cousin Russell Thompson. Now there was someone he hadn't seen in a long time. This was one of the few people he didn't mind talking to on such an important day in the life of Thompsonville. "Hi Russell," he called out to him. "Haven't seen you in a long time. Are you going to be at the big game tonight?"

Just having him say he would be there, would have done Pop a world of good. Russell was a special soul as far as Pop was concerned. Pop knew the town's well-being at times, probably rested on the huge shoulders of Russell Thompson. They had grown up together and even when they were teens, Russell had always been wise beyond his years.

The role Russell filled for Thompsonville demanded a sacrifice he was sure he and most others would never understand. If there was one person Pop wouldn't trade places with today, it was Russell Thompson.

Russell smiled and was obviously glad to see his old friend and distant relative. "Hi Ernest. Sorry. I know they call you "Coach" nowadays. No, I don't plan on making the game tonight. This is very important to you and the town and I don't want any doubts about the outcome."

Pop was intrigued by Russell's response. "Are you telling

me you know what the outcome will be?"

Russell smiled at Pop's innocent attempt to pick information. "Now Coach, if I did know the outcome, it wouldn't be fair for me to tell you and deprive you of the opportunity to experience your moment of happiness or disappointment. Now would it?"

Pop was always puzzled after having even the briefest of conversations with Russell Thompson. They talked more about old friends and relatives and promised to do some fishing together when time permitted. Pop continued his walk back to the gymnasium.

He was already in the process of packing his things to make way for the new coach (whoever that may be). He didn't have many mementos to show for his thirty plus years of coaching. He did have many memories of the players he had coached and guided into manhood.

Life didn't welcome young Negro men with open arms. All who played for Pop Thompson left with something that would be of value for their entire lives (their self-worth). His true crop was not expert basketball players, but expert young men. Of that accomplishment, he was truly proud. This is what he would miss most about the job of coaching.

It was four o'clock when he packed the last box into the pickup and started the drive home. There was a small tear in the corner of his eye as he locked his office for the last time. Angela would serve a light supper for him and Sean at 5:30pm. They would leave home at 6:30pm to go to the gymnasium.

Sean and Pop entered the gym at exactly 6:45pm. Some people were already seated in the gymnasium for the game. This game would be a sell out just as the last ten home games were. The Blue Hornets had played all of their playoff games away. This was the chance for Thompsonville High Basketball fans to witness history (a history which few in Thompsonville, and the surrounding communities intended to miss).

At 7:30, both teams were dressed and warming up. The Brooks High School Jaguars were big. Not one player on the entire team was under six feet. The Jackson Press had made them a fifteen-point favorite to win and repeat as state champions of the Negro Big 10 Conference in the state of Mississippi.

The starting five for the Thompsonville Fighting Blue Hornets were:

Albert Thompson 6′4″, Center,

Karl Johnson, 6′2″, Power Forward,

Sean Johnson 6′1″, Small Forward,

Avery Wallace 5′5″, Point Guard

Steve Wallace 5′11″, Shooting Guard.

The Blue Hornets were outsized by the Jaguars at every position.

"Okay, Coach, give me your starting five," the head referee told Pop. To his chagrin, Pop turned around to see Ed

Simmons. His face did not betray his disappointment.

"Here you are," Pop said as he handed Ed the starter's list. Ed and Pop had a history. He was not Pop's favorite official. Ed had been the Lead Official in the '55 game against Brooks.

Things didn't look good for the Fighting Blue Hornets to bring home the championship trophy. Some officials called what they saw and some called what they thought they saw. Ed was one of the latter. In Pop's mind, Ed couldn't see and Pop doubted if glasses would help. Ed had given him a technical foul in '55 when he protested a call. Pop had no intention of hurting his team that way tonight.

"Okay Team, back to the dressing room!" yelled Pop. After all the players had returned to the dressing room and gathered around him, he spoke. "This is our chance to write our names in Mississippi sports history. There may be other state championship basketball teams at Thompsonville High but you have the unique opportunity to be the first. I'm not going to lie to you and tell you it's going to be easy to beat this team. We have come a long way this season and although we only have one game left, we still have a long way to go. Let's give it the same intensity we gave the entire season. This will not just be a test of us against them, but a test of us against ourselves. Let's leave everything on the floor. Let's give it one hundred percent and, win or lose, we will be proud of ourselves. Now Albert, remember to deny the inside pass to the center when we're on defense. Avery, help him out."

Though they were small, the Blue Hornets had the stingiest zone defense of any basketball team in the Negro Big 10. With their size disadvantage, a good defensive strategy is what they would have to use against a taller Brooks the entire game.

Pop continued, "That center they have is big and strong. We didn't contain him well when we lost in Jackson. If he catches the ball inside, he'll score every time. Let's set some good picks on offense. Let's be careful with the cross court passes. Keep the game at our tempo - fast. These guys are bigger and they want a slow pace. We want to run them until their tongues are hanging out. We have the advantage in an up tempo game. I'm proud of you guys. You're the most talented team I've ever had. Let's win this game for our town, our school and ourselves."

After Pop's pep talk, Sean led the team in the Lord's Prayer. When Pop and the team reentered the gymnasium, it was full and rocking. The crowd cheered loudly as the Blue Hornets circled the gymnasium and began their final warm-ups.

After the national anthem and the Negro National anthems were played, the starting teams took the floor. As they matched up for the tip off, the size differential in favor of Brooks High was significant.

Brooks won the tip easily and began a fast break, which ended with a slam dunk. The Blue Hornets were tight. Sean missed his first two open shots and Avery had two turnovers. These errors were normally game statistics for both players and they were only thirty seconds into the game.

"Time Ref!!!" Sean said loudly after Pop had signaled to him to do so. The crowd's enthusiasm was quieted by the impressive start by the Brooks Jaguars. When the teams went back to their benches, the opposing center passed Pop and said, "Say Coach, how did this team get to the finals? Look like y'all could use some of dat *mojo* they say y'all got down here."

Of course, Pop and his team ignored the comments. He knew the game was far from over. The fans behind the bench heard the comments and responded with boos toward the opposing team.

Pop knew some serious coaching was in order. "Okay team, these guys are talking a lot of trash. Keep your cool and elevate your play to the level I know you're capable of playing at. Avery, you've got to penetrate more. You're giving up the dribble way too early. Remember what we practiced. Take the ball all the way to the hole. Your man is bigger but you're faster. Take him with your quickness. If the defense collapses on you, pass the ball outside to Sean or Steve for the open shot."

Pop had learned the new language of the court, he needed to communicate better with his team. "Now, let's run a four square on the inbounds to free Sean for the shot."

The horn sounded indicating an end to the time out. The Blue Hornets came alive. Sean did an athletic reverse slam dunk of the ball on the inbounds pass from Avery. From that point, the Blue Hornets were in the game. Brooks was now having trouble getting the ball inside to their *trash talking* center. The game was a see-saw, nip and tuck nail biting affair for the rest of the first half.

Brooks led 43-42 at half-time. Though he was playing better, Sean was still not having his usual stellar performance. Pop and the team both knew he would have to play better for Thompsonville to win this game.

Albert had three quick fouls and sat a major portion of the first half in the seat next to Pop on the bench. The backup center Wilbert "Pee Wee" Jones was a bit taller than Albert but not nearly as athletic. This would really be a problem if Albert got a quick foul in the second half. Pee Wee Jones was a good backup center. He had done okay in Albert's absence, but he did not leap as well, nor did he block shots as well as Albert though he was an inch taller.

Pop didn't talk much during halftime. He had coached as well as he could to get his team back into the game. The team appreciated his silence at halftime. It was an indication he was pleased with their effort.

Albert started the second half and Sean really came alive in the first four minutes. He was four for four from twenty feet and better. All scores were on forced turnovers. The Thompsonville gym was rocking again as the Blue Hornets surged to a seven point lead. Albert had completely stopped the Brooks center's trash talk by blocking three of his shots. The Brooks coach signaled a time-out to his team.

When the game started again, you could cut the tension in the gymnasium with a knife. Brooks defenders were all over Avery as he dribbled the basketball. He made a court-court pass to Sean, who spotted Albert under the basket. Most of the Brooks players were chasing him and Avery. Albert caught the ball and shot a lay-up which missed badly when he was hacked by Brooks' power forward. The closest referee to this action was Ed Simmons. His whistle was silent. Brooks recovered the ball from Albert's miss and started up court. Pop screamed in protest at Ed Simmons as he passed the Blue Hornets bench. Ed gave Pop his second technical foul which meant ejection from the game. Quiet fell over the crowd. Play was stopped and the Brooks point guard made the technical foul shot which tied the game.

Pop took one last opportunity to talk to his team before leaving the gymnasium. "I'm sorry I let you down," said Pop.

"I shouldn't have made that pass," said Sean.

"And I shouldn't have tried to shoot that lay up," said Albert.

"And that asshole should have called the foul," said Pop. The team each had strange looks on their faces. They had never heard a foul word uttered from their Coach's mouth.

"Okay guys, this game is in your hands now. Sean, you're our leader. Take control of the team," Pop said.

At that moment Ed Simmons was approaching the bench as if he was ready to give the team another technical foul.

"Okay, I'm outta here," said Pop.

"Who's your coach"? Ed asked.

"Sean Johnson, number seventeen is my player-coach," responded Pop as he exited the gymnasium.

The game began again. Brooks held onto the ball. Sean told his teammates not to foul. "Make them beat us with a long, outside shot," he had said.

At two seconds, number sixteen for Brooks High (their Point Guard) took a wide-open shot from fifteen feet. He had been a "knockdown shooter" all night from twenty feet. The ball actually went into the hoop and caromed out into the hands of Steve Wallace of Thompsonville High. The game clock ticked to zero. The 1964 championship game for the Mississippi Negro Big Ten Athletic Conference had gone into overtime.

Nobody knows what was said in the Fighting Blue Hornets huddle during the intermission between regulation and overtime and to this day the players won't say. When the overtime started it was no contest. The Thompsonville Fighting Hornets went on a fifteen point run to start the period. Brooks did not score a single point in the overtime. The Thompsonville partisan crowd noise was deafening.

The Blue Hornets were like mad bees who were all over the place. Albert Thompson blocked four shots, Avery Wallace had three steals. Sean Johnson had three twenty-foot rainbow jump shots and the rest of the points came on mental mistakes by Brooks from the pressure applied by the

Blue Hornets. The Jackson Press Telegram sports section reported, "There were two games in Thompsonville, Saturday night; regulation and overtime. Brooks was a valiant contender for the first game, but was clearly absent for the second one."

Pop Thompson retired as Coach at the end of that season.

He went out in style. The 1963-64 team was a team of destiny. Thompsonville would win more basketball championships, but none would ever be as sweet as the "Magic Season."

PAST MIDNIGHT
(1968-1989)

As he sat in the shadows of the darkened police station enjoying a stogie, Harvey Johnson, Jr. (sixth Chief of Police of Thompsonville Mississippi) watched the long black car slowly cruise up Main Street. It was the wee hours of the morning and he couldn't sleep. With that one exception, nothing was stirring in the town's quiet streets. He didn't see the vehicle often. It seemed he only saw it late at night when he was alone. Harvey knew it would be a futile effort to pursue it. He had succumbed to impulse and given chase once. He had followed the car as it went up Main and made a quick turn onto Washington Avenue. After Harvey made the turn, it was nowhere to be seen. He searched every alley and back street for two hours to no avail.

He had later revealed this strange encounter to Miss Mae. Miss Mae, who had run her diner since before his father was Police Chief, acknowledged familiarity with the mystery vehicle but was not forthcoming with additional information. "Let that one be, Harvey," she said. "Some things seen past midnight around here are best left alone." After those comments, Mae never spoke another word about it.

This story, however, is really about Bobby Ray Jenkins, a man who took a ride in that long black car. Bobby Ray was a talented man. He had so much talent people often said he must have sold his soul to get it. He was the richest man in Thompsonville during his time and probably, the richest Black man in Mississippi.

The nineteen eighties were coming to an end and things had changed for Black folks in America. Bobby Ray was a tall, slim good-looking fellow. He had gained his wealth as an entertainer. He was a good musician, but he was an extraordinary singer and dancer. He became rich and famous as lead singer for *The Sparrows,* the renowned rhythm and blues singing group of the late sixties and seventies. During his time, Bobby Ray was the man most women in America dreamed of when they slept at night. The Sparrows toured Europe and the world, featuring Bobby Ray Jenkins as lead singer. The group was known for its mellow five part harmonies and tight dance routines. Bobby Ray's sweet tenor voice established the trend for most of the male vocal groups of the time. In truth, he was the biggest celebrity Thompsonville ever had.

It was nineteen eighty-nine and Bobby Ray hadn't toured or

recorded a song in over a year. He now lived off investments he made with the large amount of money he made during his career. Bobby Ray always demanded cash before each performance. Checks were okay for other members of the entourage but not Bobby Ray. For as much talent as he had, he was a selfish and untrusting man. Most people in Thompsonville didn't care much for him as a person. "I knew him when he was in high school," said Eddie Thompson. Eddie was an old timer who had been a regular at Mae's Diner for years. "Damnedest thing you ever seen. His whole face was one big pimple and he couldn't dance a lick. His knees knocked so bad you could hear em, and he had a bit of a stutter. The next thing I hear he's cut a record with a big time New Orleans record company. They tell me The Sparrows was just a local singing group trying to be like the Temptations or somebody, but just barely g'tting' gigs in New Orleans. Get this. Their lead singer is shot and killed in a liquor store robbery on Chef Menteur Highway. Who replaces him? Bobby Ray. The rest is history." *Stay With My Baby* was their first hit. It went gold inside six weeks. They had twelve mo after that one. It's not natural I tell you." The story Eddie Thompson was telling stopped abruptly as Bobby Ray entered the diner.

Bobby Ray still sported the pompadour hairstyle he had worn since he first began his career. It seemed somewhat out of place among the more contemporary hairstyles worn by the male patrons in Mae's Diner. His still smooth handsome face was hidden behind dark sunglasses. The bright light inside the diner caused his gold capped tooth with the diamond stud to sparkle.

Bobby Ray became an even bigger star after he left the Sparrows to go solo. The license plate on his Bentley was personalized. It spelled "T-r-u-d-y" which was the title of his first million seller as a solo artist.

A young fan in the diner was collared abruptly by a watchful parent as he approached Bobby Ray for an autograph. Most everyone in town knew better than to ask. Bobby Ray no longer signed autographs. He hardly spoke except to order from the menu. He sat alone in the back booth whenever he came to the diner. He would offer his usual fake smile, but never ever carried on a conversation with patrons of the diner. He would quietly eat his meal, leave Mae a five dollar tip and nod to his chauffeur when he was ready to leave. Although he was the richest man around, he was not a benefactor, in any way, to the Thompsonville community. He was only concerned with the needs of Bobby Ray Jenkins.

After he left, the diner conversation began again. "It's just like I always say," spoke Rudy Thompson (another regular of the diner). "A greedy man can't enter the Kingdom. You never see that boy in church. He never donates nothing to our community or our schools. He can't take all that money wid him. Ain't no undertaker in the world gonna let him outta here with one red dime."

A mild chuckle rumbled through the diner patronage. Eddie Thompson seconded Rudy's comment. "You can say that again," he said with a strange smile.

Such was the talk around town about Bobby Ray Jenkins. For a man with all his fame and wealth, he was not a model citizen in his own hometown. Bobby Ray reflected back on his ride in the long black car. It was his nineteenth birthday. It was July 5th, 1969. As a teenager growing up in rural Mississippi, he had absolutely nothing going on in his life. He had a bad complexion, nappy hair and he only weighed one hundred thirty-five pounds soaking wet, even though he was six feet two inches tall. He was an only child. His great aunt Minnie Thompson, who everybody called Aunt Minnie, adopted him. His parents up and left Thompsonville one day when he was only six weeks old and left him on Aunt Minnie's front porch. She was a middle-aged spinster who never married or had children, but she had plenty love in her heart for Bobby Ray. She raised him without complaint.

He had a few friends growing up, but he was mostly a loner. He was just a C plus student and showed no specific interests or talents to speak of. Aunt Minnie encouraged him to join the Army when he graduated high school. He had given serious thought to that idea until he took that ride. He drank wine down by the creek with some of the neighborhood *toughs* during his summers in high school. Aunt Minnie had often warned him about staying out late, especially during the hot summer months. He never took her warnings seriously. To Bobby Ray, she was just an old woman who was superstitious and scared of everything.

As a teenager, Bobby Ray wasn't particularly attractive to the girls so, hanging out late and getting high on cheap wine was *above average* entertainment. He and his drinking buddies usually got one of the town drunks to go inside the package store to make their purchase since they were all under age. They would offer fifty cents and most times the person they asked would be more than glad to consummate the sale for them.

One summer night after a sharing a pint of port with two other boys down at the creek, Bobby Ray was heading home to the quarters. He was accustomed to making the quiet walk home alone. It gave him time to come up with the excuse he would give Aunt Minnie if she were still up waiting for him. He was walking up Main Street when the big car startled him as it approached. As it slowed to a stop, Bobby Ray's face was even with the rear passenger door window. Though he was no more than two feet away from the car its windows were so dark he could not see who was inside. The passenger door opened slowly and a large hairy hand with long nails and bony fingers beckoned him to get inside. He thought for a second, then fearfully obliged. As he remembered, he was sure it was the cheap wine that gave him the courage to get into the car.

The following morning after his ride, Bobby Ray awoke to see a stranger in the mirror. His face was almost smooth. He still looked the same, but the mirror reflected a much better looking version of his previous self. Every day, thereafter, brought some minor change for the better that he noticed. Apparently, so did the girls because he got at least three telephone calls from girls each night asking dumb questions about the town picnic, or other silly things, just to get the chance to talk to him. He was keenly aware of the pact he made. The man in the Black car had told him to expect this. He was not afraid of many things in life, but when he remembered his encounter with the man in the back of the

Black car it almost made his skin crawl.

Bobby liked pretty women, but he knew they would still be available after he took care of those things he desired most. One catch to the deal he made was he must always live in Thompsonville. He must maintain his residence there and could not stay away for an extended period of time. That wasn't necessarily his preference since he had no ties here, other than Aunt Minnie. Besides, according to the man in the Black car she wouldn't be around much longer. Though he always dreamed of leaving Mississippi and never returning, living in Thompsonville was a small price to pay for what he would receive in return.

Two weeks after his ride, Bobby Ray entered his first talent show at the Thompsonville Community Center. He did a dance routine to a James Brown dance tune. He was light on his feet as he had never been before. He did James Brown's dance routines better than James Brown. He was the unanimous winner and thus began the entertainment career of Bobby Ray Jenkins.

That talent show was almost twenty years ago. Bobby Ray was now thirty-nine. He still had his good looks, his style and (most of all) his talent. He never believed he could agree to sell his soul for any reason, but when talent was offered the temptation was too great. He had always wanted to be adored and famous. During the past twenty years, he never considered marriage. He found out he could only love himself. He had nothing to offer a woman on a full time basis. He had traveled the world and performed for kings and queens. What was there now left to do? He had built his mansion just a mile from downtown. It was worth at least two million dollars and it was one of the most expensive residential properties in Mississippi.

Bobby Ray had a single enemy - *time*. He had encountered the black car only once since he signed the contract. That was after a house rocking performance in Tokyo. He had done three encores and closed the show with a twenty-minute version of "Trudy". After the performance, he wondered, aloud, if he should move to Japan and forget the pact he made in the Big Black car that night. As he exited the theatre to get to his limousine in the dark alley behind the building, he saw the black car approach and block his limo's exit. He never doubted it was the same vehicle. Even after such a high-energy performance, his heart was racing at a million beats a minute as he broke into a cold sweat and vowed never to even think about living anywhere other than Thompsonville. He blinked, and when he opened his eyes, the Black car seemed to have vanished in that short instant.

Bobby Ray Jenkins had purchased twenty years of fame and fortune. The price was his immortal soul. He had danced the dance and now it was time to pay up. By his estimate, he had less than thirty days remaining. He had taken his ride in July of 1969. It was now June 5th, 1989.

He wasn't sure what he really had to fear. The whole thing may have been some sort of dream or illusion. He couldn't deny his sudden good looks, his talent and certainly not his money. Most people never got the entire package and if they did, they were born with it. They weren't transformed on their nineteeh birthday as dramatically as Bobby Ray had been. He knew, in his heart, he had cheated to get his, and cheaters always lose.

He constantly thought of ideas to remove himself from his dire situation. It was quietly spoken that certain folks around town could help a person get past some of the misery of their lives. Russell and William Thompson (he had heard) could do certain things. William was a only few years older than Bobby Ray. Russell, who was old enough to be his father was William's older cousin. It was said he had helped William bring his *so say* mystic talents to the fore.

Bobby Ray approached Russell one night as he left Mae's Diner. As he got out of his car and walked toward him Russell did not even acknowledge his presence and moved quickly to the other side of the street. It was if he could smell the evil that was upon him and wanted no part of it. Bobby Ray never had that problem. He usually had to have his chauffeur and bodyguard prevent people from intruding on his privacy. He was perturbed that Russell refused to even acknowledge he existed.

He gazed into the fireplace of his den as he sipped a glass of Chablis before retiring. He would sleep alone again tonight as he had for the past three weeks. The anxiety created by the twenty-year anniversary of his ride left him less than desirous of female companionship. Bobby Ray had more than made up for what he missed socially in high school. He hadn't met a woman he couldn't have. It was more than his money. There was also something about being an entertainer that turned women on. They were attracted to Bobby Ray like bears were attracted to honey. He gazed at the picture of him and the Sparrows performing on stage at the New Orleans Superdome. He had pulled the finest babe in the house that night and took her back to his swank hotel room that overlooked the river for a nightcap and breakfast in bed.

He had a career of memories on the wall of his study. Willie Strong and Bobby Ray were rival members of the Sparrows. Willie sang a mellow and soulful baritone and actually sang lead on one of the Sparrows hits that went gold. He and Bobby Ray would argue all the time, but when the stage lights hit them the Sparrows were together. They were in tune and in step. You would never guess Bobby Ray and Willie couldn't actually stand each other. This was, of course, before the days of the supermarket tabloid papers that knew all and told all. The celebrity image of the Sparrows had always been squeaky clean, however, Willie Strong didn't try to withhold his enthusiasm when Bobby Ray decided to go solo. Bobby Ray wished the Sparrows well and his career never missed a beat.

Willie Strong got his chance to be lead singer for the Sparrows and no less than six months after Bobby Ray's departure, the Sparrows produced and distributed "The Best of The Sparrows" which signaled their demise as a major rhythm and blues group. On the other hand, Bobby Ray's career continued to soar for another ten years.

Bobby quietly went into unofficial retirement after nineteen years in the business. Producers still called, though not as frequently as they had during the first six months, trying to encourage him to do new projects or go on tour. Bobby Ray refused each and every offer. The word was out that he had quit and become a recluse. Bobby didn't care. He had to prepare himself for his date with destiny. Luckily, Will Thompson was in town and could be Bobby Ray's last chance. Will agreed to meet him in Dora Jane Park, downtown by the lake. He was surprised that Will had returned his call after his Cousin Russell refused to even acknowledge his presence.

It was a typical summer afternoon in Thompsonville. Dora Jane Park was the beautiful memorial park in the Town Square. There were beautiful flowers and a reflection pool where many species of birds gathered in the afternoon.

Bobby Ray's Bentley stopped at the corner and he got out and walked toward the area of the park where William Thompson was seated. Will seemed quite at ease as he drank in the warm afternoon breeze and fed the birds. His style was quite a contrast to the slick, smooth entertainer image projected by Bobby Ray. He was wearing a white sport shirt and dress slacks. He rose to meet Bobby Ray. Bobby Ray was more humble than he had been in years as he greeted Will Thompson. "Thank You Mr. Thompson for seeing me," he said.

Will was forties aged and slightly gray. He was a clean cut and fit looking black man. Bobby Ray had never met him personally. Because he was a few years older than Bobby Ray, they had only crossed paths occasionally when he was a youngster growing up. Though he had been gone many years and had moved to Arizona, William Thompson was still a much respected man in Thompsonville. In certain circles, William Thompson was the most famous person from Thompsonville.

"It's also good to finally meet you Bobby Ray. I'll have you know, I have the entire collection from the Sparrows."

Bobby let an uncomfortable half smile. "It's good to know you're a fan Mr. Thompson but that's not why I'm here."

Will changed gears from the ice-breaking small talk. "I know that's not why you're here. I have some idea, but why don't you tell me."

Bobby Ray looked uncomfortable as if he were expecting someone or something he really didn't care to overhear their conversation.

"I can tell you this," said Will in an effort to put him at ease. "You have nothing to fear right here and right now."

Bobby Ray began to tell Will of his encounter so long ago with the big, black car and the strange passenger inside. "……and his eyes were yellowish. They looked like cat eyes. He had long bony fingers and slightly pointed ears. He was scary as hell. As soon as I sat down in the back seat and I saw who had invited me inside, I wanted to run from that car as fast as I could, but something made me sit down and kept me inside. I was kind of paralyzed with both fear and expectation. It was obvious he was a Black man and he was old. His skin was wrinkled and there was something sinister and evil about him. Even though he smelled evil, he quickly made promises that kept my attention and calmed my fears. He asked what I most desired which intrigued me. Then he promised to give that and more to me for a small price. To humor him, I asked for fame and fortune, good looks, you know ordinary things that most folks want. I had no idea this guy could deliver, but his price was steep; my immortal soul. In return he would give me twenty years of what I asked for and then he would collect. For a nineteen year old boy twenty years is an eternity, and it didn't look like that fellow would possibly live long enough to collect (even if this was a legitimate deal)."

Will looked at Bobby Ray with an arched eyebrow and spoke seriously for the first time since he began. "I can assure you this. It was a legitimate deal and he is still around waiting to collect." Finally someone gave testament that he wasn't crazy and more importantly validated the seriousness of the transaction he had entered. Will continued. "Just because a person believes certain things are fantasy doesn't make them so. There are many things under the sun not written or spoken which affect every moment and circumstance of our lives. The occupant of that black car is known as *"a Harvester of souls."* He is constantly seeking unsuspecting and unbelieving persons such as yourself who are looking for a shortcut."

Bobby Ray was very attentive to Will's description of the man in the black car. Perhaps, at last he would find out exactly what it was he entered into when he got into the that car. "Did he have you sign anything?" Will asked.

"He had this written contract which I didn't read in detail, but its content seemed general in nature. I signed in blood with this quill pen. The old fool pricked my right index finger to get the blood for me to write my signature. My finger still stings, at times, to this day. He had this wicked smile of satisfaction on his face after I signed the contract. He gave me a hundred-dollar bill and told me to get me some nice clothes which he said I would need in the near future. I used that money plus the money I won in the Thompsonville talent show to get to New Orleans to perform at the Saenger Theatre's "Crescent City Amateur Talent Showcase". As you know, I still live in Thompsonville even though I have no friends here anymore or any other ties. I have always kept an apartment in New Orleans to use when I was recording or rehearsing. I would have left here a long time ago had I been able.

"My aunt Minnie died two years after I found success with the Sparrows. She never treated me the same after my change. In her heart, she knew something about me was different. I offered to build her a house after I had gotten some good paydays but she wouldn't accept. She never used any of the money I put in a special bank account for her. She told me she wanted no part of the Satan's money and said she prayed mightily for my soul every night. I never told her anything about what happened to me, but I believe somehow in her heart she knew."

Will was shaking his head slightly as Bobby Ray finished his story. "You know Bobby Ray, you should consider yourself blessed in some respects. This great little town we live in, Thompsonville, is a powerful place. The fact that you live here may be the one thing that may help resolve some the issues of the dire situation you now find yourself in. My Cousin Russell and I talked about you after you contacted me. He has never had the desire to involve himself in certain elements of the dark side. That's why he will never even speak to someone in your present situation. I will offer you what help I can but, to be honest, you're up against powerful forces. One important point is obvious. You entered of your own volition into a binding contract for your soul."

Bobby Ray then asked Will a serious question. "Do you or your Cousin Russell know this man? Is he the devil?"

Will responded. "Yes, we both are familiar with the man you signed your contract with."

"Is he the Prince of Darkness?"

"No, but he is indeed an emissary. This evil has plagued our family since slavery times. The man you met is probably Tyler Thompson. He was a slave on the old Thompson Plantation in Georgia."

Bobby Ray was puzzled by this explanation. "But that would make him well over one hundred years old."

Will quickly replied, "Truth is, according to Russell, he's much older than that. He and Dora Jane (this town's slave mother), were brother and sister growing up on the Thompson Georgia Plantation. Remember, God created both light and darkness. Dora Jane chose light. Her brother Tyler chose darkness. The spells he conjures have kept him around long past his allotted time. He feeds on the souls of others to maintain his longevity. The person you saw in the car is the real Tyler. He exists most times behind a mask. He has an alternate everyday identity. In that identity, he appears no different than you or I. Who he is, none of us really know for sure. He will only come to those who request his services. Perhaps, sometime during the times you drank wine with your buddies during your youth down by the creek you indicated you would sell your soul to be rich and famous. Tyler must have heard your wish and made his services available to you. The things we say, even in jest, are taken seriously by certain forces we are not even aware of. It sounds like you have a contract that is nearing its payoff. Can I or my Cousin Russell help? I'm not sure. I am willing to do what I can but when it's all said and done, it's all up to you.

"I've accepted my role in life as a teacher and counselor and because I've done so it is my duty to help you if I can. That is why I'm here. I have brought you two things which may be of value to you. Here is a book and an amulet. Both have been in the Thompson family for many generations. Perhaps you can find something in these to help you through your dilemma. The only choice you have is to honor your appointment with the man in the black car. That is also your only chance to save your soul. Those who have sought to flee have done so to no avail, and have lost their souls to Tyler Thompson or his kind.

"During the time you have left, you better pray, read the book I have given you and find time to meditate and strengthen your spirit. The amulet I have given you will help you do that. Perhaps, just perhaps, you can save yourself. This is all myself, Russell or anyone else can do for you."

With that last comment, Will got up from the park bench and walked slowly away never looking back toward Bobby Ray Jenkins.

Bobby Ray looked at the book. It was worn and tattered. Its title was *Book of Spells and Invocations.* It was obviously a hand written translation from a language he could not even guess. The amulet was that of a tribal warrior. It was a set inside a metal casing that was worn smooth by the years, but something about it felt comforting. Bobby Ray could feel its power.

He read the book Will gave him from cover to cover over the next few weeks as he awaited his date with the black car. He prayed day and night. He even graced the First Baptist Church with his presence for two consecutive Sunday services where he left checks totaling two thousand dollars in the collection plate. Bobby Ray had learned some things during the past weeks and was very thankful for the help and support Will had provided.

He prayed and meditated daily with the amulet as Will had suggested. He may not be able to save his soul, but with the knowledge he had gained since he met Will Thompson, he believed he was a changed person and that gave him hope.

It was 11:45pm on July eighth. All of the estate staff had gone home for the night including Willie his chauffeur. Bobby Ray had readied himself for his appointment. He exited the house and began his walk toward town. Walking would give him time to steady his nerves and prepare for whatever his fate would be. Traffic was light as he made the walk into town. As he glanced at his Rolex, it was 12:30am. Main Street was as quiet as it had been twenty years ago. Downtown had changed significantly over the years, however, he remembered exactly where he encountered the black car.

As he made his way to the corner of Main and Chestnut, he could hear the noise of the familiar vehicle's tires break the silence of the quiet early morning. Bobby Ray looked back and could not disguise the fear in his eyes as the car stopped and its passenger door opened. Bobby Ray quietly gathered himself counted to ten and stepped inside. It was as if he had stepped twenty years back into the past. The car was the same. What was different was the creepy old man. He didn't seem as old as before. His eyes were still yellowish and cat like and his ears were slightly pointy as before. Somewhere between 1969 and 1989 he had lost twenty years as Bobby Ray had gained twenty. From his research Bobby Ray knew this was the illusion created by the soul stealing Tyler Thompson. Tyler's eyes were eager with the anticipation of the harvest. The jar sat on the seat next to him that held the souls of those who had paid their due.

"Step in Mr. Jenkins," he said in a sinister voice. Soon his expression of anticipation quickly changed to that of discomfort and disgust. "I see William Thompson has given you something. It won't do you any good." Tyler angrily snatched the amulet from Bobby Ray's neck, rolled the window down slightly and tossed it from the car.

Something else about Tyler was different. Bobby Ray couldn't quite put his finger on it, but Tyler vaguely reminded him of someone else. If only he could remember.

"It's time to pay your fee Mr. Jenkins."

Bobby Ray had learned quite a bit since he met Will Thompson in the park that day. "I claim the right of refusal," he spoke in a bold and confident voice.

Tyler's reaction to those words was more severe than his reaction to the amulet Bobby Ray wore. "And who, pray tell has introduced you to the *Book of Spells and Invocations*? A little learning is a dangerous thing Mr. Jenkins. I hope you know the significance of the words you have just spoken."

Bobby Ray was bolder now. He knew his words had bought him some time.

"The spell you have cast for the rights to my soul gives me the right of refusal," Bobby Ray said.

"I have a contract signed by you and me Mr. Jenkins," Tyler Thompson sneered. "Nothing you can do will erase the terms of the contract."

Bobby Ray had read the spell to claim the soul of another fifty different times since he received the book from Will Thompson. Certain passages did apply to his situation. If the one whose soul has been bartered, has any true faith in God or any good at all left in them, they may claim the "Right of Refusal". He knew before he met Will Thompson, he could make no such claim and would have had to willingly surrender his soul to Tyler without a fight. The book further stated, "Whoever claimed this right must have the purity of heart necessary to survive the challenge of the Soul Harvester."

Bobby had meditated many hours with the amulet. His resolve was strong. Tyler was outraged with the claim Bobby Ray made. "You know you have challenged me Mr. Jenkins and it will be a contest of wills to the death for one of us."

If one was able to win this challenge it would send the soul of the soul harvester to oblivion and all of the souls he had claimed would be released to freely find the light. If he lost, however, he would be one of those wretched beings captured in the jar of swirling blue and black mist and in possession of the ghoul, demon or warlock as they were sometimes called.

Bobby returned his stare without fear. Whatever the outcome of this battle, he was prepared to accept. "I gladly accept this challenge. I seek to do mankind a favor. I will gladly give up all you have given me, talent, fame, riches to see the world rid of you."

That further infuriated Tyler. The book said renouncing what he had received would give him further strength for his challenge. Tyler also knew that. He had never had a human being challenge his right to claim his soul. *"Damn William and Russell Thompson."* In a fit of anger, Tyler raised his hand above his head and the dance began. He would show this poor excuse of a human being what fate came to those who had the audacity to challenge his right to claim his soul.

Tyler's long fingernails appeared razor sharp. One crisp swipe across Bobby Ray's neck and it would be over in an instant. Bobby Ray's research told him these warlocks were extremely strong and their sharp nails could snuff out a man's life with one stroke. He closed his eyes as the weapon that was Tyler's right hand descended with a mighty force toward his neck. He waited. He waited and waited and waited. He never opened his eyes. The African Book of Spells and Invocations said, "If a man's resolve was strong enough and long enough he could win. But if he had even the slightest of doubt his life would be in grave danger". Most men weren't strong enough to withstand the mental intimidation of a ghoul who had the power to harvest a man's soul. Bobby Ray's meditation had paid off. He held his eyes shut tight and his mind was clear and strong, but he knew he would have to maintain longer, much longer.

Ever so slightly his concentration began to drift. This was like trying to hold your breath for an hour. Though his mind was beginning to lose focus, he could still feel he was winning the mental tug of war required to defeat this vile creature. He felt himself weakening. He could no longer resist the temptation to open his eyes. The book said, *"To open one's eyes could mean certain death and the loss of one's soul for eternity."* Just a little longer. He was mentally exhausted and when he could no longer resist, he opened his left eye just in time to see the ghoulish hand with deadly sharp talons descending toward his neck in slow motion.

He was able to move his head just far enough to prevent his jugular vein from being severed. Instead, he received a long scratch as the ghoul's hand separated from its wrist as it grazed his neck and hit the floor of the car with a thud. It was the last move the dying creature made. Bobby Ray had challenged and won the intense struggle of wills.

The ghoul's hand slowly dissolved into sand. Tyler's face showed intense pain and aged rapidly before his very eyes. He completely disintegrated and turned first into rotting flesh and then into a pile of dirt on the seat of the black car. Bobby Ray could feel warm blood rolling from his neck into his shirt.

Preparation had saved his life. He saw the souls of others release themselves from the jar on the seat next to what had been Tyler Thompson. Tiny beams of light soared from the car and out into the dark night. Humanity was rid of a parasite who preyed on the unknowing and the unsuspecting. Bobby Ray would have willingly paid a price greater than the scratch on his neck for his freedom.

Inexplicably, the gold capped tooth fell from his mouth and hit the pavement as he exited the car and began his walk home. He didn't even bother to pick it up. He could feel the heat from the big black car as it was consumed by flames. He didn't even bother to look back. He spotted Will's amulet on the sidewalk near Chestnut and Main where Tyler had tossed it. He retrieved it and put it in his pocket. He would return it to Will Thompson.

Daylight found him with his car fully packed. He would take the sedan so as not to draw much attention. He would leave this town today and never return. He knew if he stayed, he'd have a lot of explaining to do.

The tall skinny knock-kneed man entered the diner and sat

at the counter. He was slightly balding, appeared to be around forty and had a bad complexion. "Cofffeee...please" he stuttered.

Mae quickly obliged. She noticed he had a bandage on his neck. "Hurt yourself shaving?" she said.

"Suure did," he said. Do yooou know Mr. Will Thompson?"

Mae replied "Sure, I know him."

The man said, "I'mmm... just passin throoogh and I'm in a hurry. Can I.....leave something here for him?"

This guy looked harmless enough, though there was something familiar about him she couldn't place. "Sure, what is it?"

The man produced the amulet of the African Warrior and a book, which was wrapped in brown paper. "I realllly appreciate thththis," he said.

"No problem. You should consider yourself lucky. All you've got is a razor scratch. Eddie Thompson, one of our longtime regulars around here, was found dead in the middle of Main Street early this morning. Chief Harvey Thomson told me the coroner said he had a massive heart attack. What a place to be when your number is called."

A look of surprise came on the stranger's face. "Welllll.... Thanks very much Mam. I gottgotta be goin'." The stranger left a five-dollar tip on the counter even though he only had coffee.

As he drove down the highway, he reflected on the events of the past twenty years. He had given up a lot for what he received in the back seat of the black car. Tears came to his eyes as he realized he had taken the love his Aunt Minnie had selflessly given him all those years for granted. He hoped he would one day get a chance to make that up to her, perhaps in the great beyond. He wiped his tears and composed himself. He felt as if he had learned more about life and living in the past thirty days than he had during the past thirty years. Leaving home for good would be a new adventure that he welcomed with open arms.

AVONELLA
(1986)

Avonella Thompson was not the kind of woman a man could use and abuse. She had come a long way from her hometown of Thompsonville, Mississippi and she had no desire to go back. She had a good job in the New Orleans Business District that paid her over $50,000 a year. That was more money than anyone in her entire family had ever earned in a single year. She was that rare five feet six inches, "Brown Bomber" with smooth skin and long wavy hair. She was well educated. She had received her MBA from Tulane University. She was a very beautiful and headstrong woman.

Her weakness was and had always been her male relationships. It seemed she was just a bit unlucky. Perhaps it was her gorgeous presence that intimidated the men she felt were the best matrimonial candidates.

Her present situation was perplexing. She had really dropped her guard and everything else for her latest beau. He was one of those exceptional guys who didn't seem intimidated by her aura and before she knew it she was deeply in love with him.

Avonella was thirty two years old and had never been married. Two of her sisters, Authurine and Gladys, were married. Her youngest sister, Patricia was not married but had three children by three different men. Avonella was sure that would not happen to her.

At first, she believed this man was her knight, her savior. She had already gotten a first rate education, landed a good job, and had a nice home in suburban Metairie. The last jewel in her crown was a man, a good man, not a dog. Lord knows, she had already been through enough of them. This guy represented her truly uplifting herself from the poor condition into which she was born.

She couldn't have been more wrong. She thought she-had a great relationship with Clarence which added further insult to the injury his behavior had caused. He dropped her cold when he found out about the baby.

She had surrendered herself to him. Maybe too soon she thought, which may have been why he walked away. He told her (on more than one occasion) he wasn't ready for commitment. Her pregnancy was the last straw. He had written her a check for five hundred dollars and told her to get rid of it. Tears flowed down her cheeks as she recalled the coldness of that act.

Clarence signaled to the bartender to fill both glasses with another round. "So, what do you like to do in your spare time?" Was the question he posed to the pretty young Creole woman on the bar stool next to him.

Clarence was a player who had a weakness for pretty women, though he lost interest in them after a brief time. He tired of the same woman quickly. He was an extremely handsome and charming man. He had no trouble attracting or keeping women.

Avonella had just gotten the wrong idea. He knew he stayed a little too long with her. It was probably because she had such a strong will. Most men find it hard to resist that challenge. Clarence P. Goodnight was no exception. After his conquest of her, he found himself treating her just like all of the rest. He wearied of her pushy and demanding attitude. It was obvious she was looking for a husband. He knew that was not a role he wanted to play soon. Clarence paid the bar tab and he and the latest candidate were heading to his apartment.

"I told you that *Negro* was a ladies' man the first time I saw him," said Carole (Avonella's best friend). They were having coffee and danish in the company cafeteria. "He probably had a few women on the side all along."

Avonella knew she was probably right and could only kick herself for believing otherwise. She was now in a situation she never wanted to be in; pregnant without a man at her side. She was a good-looking woman, but there were thousands of women in New Orleans who were just as pretty, looking for husbands who weren't pregnant.

That, however, was not where her mind was. Avonella's major concern now was how she could exact vengeance on that *no account scoundrel* Clarence Philip Goodnight. He had stopped calling and would not return her calls or even answer his phone. He had to know she wanted to talk, especially after the letter she hand delivered to his house. Well Mr. Goodnight had really underestimated the limits of her determination. She was not a quitter. This was New Orleans and she still had one more thing she would try.

Ms. Rochelle was attired in a red head rag with a corncob pipe extended from her thick black lips. "Come in chile," she spoke in a friendly voice. Her voice sounded a little different in person. It was not easy to tell how old she was, but Avonella guessed she must be late fifties or early sixties. She was dark and rotund. Though she was large, she was not excessively fat, but firm, as if she was no stranger to hard work. She invited Avonella into her shotgun house. Avonella was slightly uncomfortable parking her car on the street in this part of Uptown.

This was a very rough area of New Orleans. A group of young toughs loitered on the corner across from Ms. Rochelle's house. Ms. Rochelle could see Avonella's discomfort as she peered back at her sporty BMW.

"Don't you worry," she said as if she had read her mind. "That street trash would rather do a lot of other things than mess with any of my guests' property."

She invited Avonella in and offered her a seat in a large comfortable chair which she accepted. Miss Rochelle sat at the dining room table. The room was dimly lit and smelled of the kerosene that powered the single lamp. "I still don't likes too much 'lectricity in my house. So, you got man trouble, huh? Well, what can Miss Rochelle give you Honey? Justice, vengence, satisfactshun, all of dat?" she asked.

Avonella could only nod her head. The pain, this man had caused her, was great. "Say it chile! Say it out loud!" Ms. Rochelle brought her a cup of hot mint tea with honey and lemon. Even though it was a warm Louisiana evening, the tea soothed her emotions and allowed her to clear her head. She finally was able to answer Miss Rochelle's question. "I want him to suffer as I have suffered. I deserve much more than he has given me."

Ms. Rochelle smiled, looked her in the eye and asked, "Did you bring what I asked?"

Ms. Rochelle's eyes had a slightly wild look as she waited in anticipation. Avonella slowly removed the mason jars from her purse and looked away as she placed them on the table. Hers' was a strange request. Ms. Rochelle had asked for the eye of a frog, the testicles of a stray dog and three marbles stolen from a six year old male child (plus, of course, $500 dollars cash in old bills).

Very few six year old boys still played marbles. A fellow her friend Carole knew, who worked at the Animal Control Bureau out in New Orleans East, had secured the testicles for her for twenty dollars.

"Ugh!" she moaned as she handed them to Ms. Rochelle in the second jar. She had gotten the frog's eye from her neighbor (a high school biology student). The marbles were somewhat tricky. She had actually bought some for her

nephew, *Little Tiny,* and actually took three from the pack without his permission. Lastly, she put the cash on the table next to the jars. Ms. Rochelle's request had tested her principles, but her act of vengeance toward Clarence was itself a challenge to those principles. Ms. Rochelle's face betrayed a bit of a frown as she said, "I guess I'll accept the marbles." She quickly grabbed the five one hundred-dollar bills, stacked them up and deposited them into a well worn leather bag.

"Be right back," she said. She returned after what seemed like thirty minutes with a small baby food jar full of a greenish paste. She handed it to Avonella and proceeded to give her specific directions. "Put this anyplace he may put his hands. Spread it lightly wid a soff toothbrush. Put it on his do nobs, car dos and so forth. It don't take much. You gon get your satisfactshun in bout six weeks." Avonella didn't ask what was in the jar and really didn't want to know. All she knew was she was getting what she wanted, "Revenge!!"

Clarence looked into the mirror. He frequently talked to himself while shaving or combing his hair. "You are one fine man, Clarence Philip Goodnight" he said. "No wonder women can't get enough of you." He believed those words in his heart. He knew he was a good catch for any woman in New Orleans. He came from a good family, was a graduate of Tulane Law School and had a promising career with one of the oldest and most prestigious Law firms in New

Orleans. He was handsome, had wavy hair and that smooth Uptown New Orleans "coffee au lait" complexion. His friends sometimes told him he looked like a White man with a deep tan. Most "dark-skinned" Black women were at his mercy. He hadn't seen one he couldn't get. The darker they were, the easier they were. He often wondered why that was. He was sure it was some deep psychological issue.

He laughed out loud thinking about Avonella. She was as dark a girl as he had ever dated. She was a smart Mississippi country girl who had overcome. She was worth having because she was pretty. She was worth keeping for a while anyway, that is, until she told him she was pregnant.

Clarence took one more look in the mirror as he adjusted his tie. He grabbed his briefcase and headed out the door of his fashionable townhouse apartment. *What was this grease on the handle of his car*? He wiped it off his hands with the white handkerchief in his suit pocket. He always paid good money to keep his Mercedes detailed. It really pissed him off that someone, possibly a valet, had neglected to clean their hands before parking his car.

Three weeks had passed since Avonella followed Ms. Rochelle's directions and carefully placed the substance where Clarence would contact it. As Clarence peered into the mirror during his morning ritual, he noticed how slow his beard was growing. As of late, he could go three days without having to shave. That was odd.

He also remembered the most unusual thing that happened to him at the YMCA the other day. For the briefest instant in the shower, he had glimpsed his racquetball partner, Andre Richard, naked and the image of Andre's naked body stimulated him sexually. That couldn't possibly be. He was all man. He had never had a homosexual encounter nor did he long to. He figured it must have been just an aberration and forgot the incident.

Clarence was really distressed after he and Monique, his latest conquest, finished making love. He must be imagining this, but he seemed to have lost some size in his groin area. Monique brought it to his attention. "What's the matter honey? Don't I excite you anymore?" Clarence was so upset, he made an appointment to see his doctor the next day.

Dr. Drexel had been his doctor as long as he could remember. He was a long-time family friend and treated him like his own son. "Look, Clarence this is probably just nervous anxiety. You'd be surprised how stress can affect all aspects of your life." He prescribed stress medication for him.

After a week of the medication, Clarence didn't notice any change in his condition. He was really scared now. He noticed his breasts were very sensitive and both had unusual swelling. He had an incredible and an inexplicable urge to wear women's clothes. He bought feminine underwear, high heels and cosmetics and modeled in the full-length mirror of his bathroom. He became less and less interested in Monique or any other woman. Andre, his racquetball partner had mentioned jokingly that his ass was really soft and feminine looking and told him he needed to get more exercise. He had always worn his hair a little long and in "image conscious" New Orleans, his appearance was now pushing the envelope of acceptability for the Law firm. Clarence's problem was starting to become noticeable. A week after Andre's comment, he looked at himself in the mirror and what looked back was a fabulous looking female.

He took great pains to try to continue to look masculine, but to no avail. He heard the whispers in the office about hormonal problems. It was surely just a matter of time before CJ, the firm's senior partner, broached the subject with him. His walk had definitely become feminine. At least two of the male staff employees had made passes at him.

Dr. Drexel, nor any of the other specialists he had been referred to, didn't have any answers. His penis now measured only one inch long. He had a thirty-eight D cup bra size. He wore large baggy clothing in a futile effort to disguise his condition. His beard and his mustache were completely gone. He looked, for all practical purposes, female.

The emotional turmoil this metamorphosis was causing was immense. He had fits of crying and did not answer his phone. He tried to avoid his family at all costs. He had been ordered on a forced leave of absence from his firm until his condition cleared up.

Clarence was not even a shadow of the "lady killer," he had once been. This particular morning he awakened to something new and different between his legs. This was the last straw. He fell into a fit of crying that was only interrupted by the persistent ring of his doorbell. He had tried to avoid seeing anyone after his condition got severe but he was so distraught he answered the door, hoping whoever it was could give him comfort. To his amazement, it was Avonella. He had not given one thought to her during his past few weeks of turmoil.

They both looked surprised. Avonella knew at that moment how her revenge had been exacted. By the half smile on her face, Clarence also now knew who was responsible for this terrible spell that was put on him. This was New Orleans and Clarence knew there were those who could cast a spell on you if the asking price was paid. "Why have you done this to me?" he sobbed.

"Why did you do what you did to me?" she responded. "I'm pregnant and you know it's yours," she said.

A repentant Clarence responded. "I'm truly sorry. I'll do anything. Just change me back."

"Anything?" she responded. "Well, okay," she said. "Sign this."

Through tearful eyes, Clarence hesitated, then signed the document she presented without even reading it. What he signed was a statement admitting paternity of her child and an intent of marriage to Avonella. Though the legality of her document could be in question, it was a moot point. What Clarence wanted now was relief; to be a man again, no matter what the cost. For Avonella, this was the *coup de gras.*

Six months later, New Orleans had the most unusual wedding. Though it was one of the largest weddings of the year, it was not covered by the society pages of the city's major newspaper which, in itself, was very unusual. In local social circles, it was whispered that royalty was marrying a commoner with Clarence Goodnight of the Uptown Goodnights marrying Avonella Thompson (a nobody from Mississippi).

Avonella was a beautiful "pregnant" bride in her white flowing wedding gown. Clarence, impeccably dressed in formal attire, had a contented, but, somewhat scary look that belied the attitude he showed toward the institution of marriage just a few months earlier.

Ms. Rochelle charged Avonella exactly $1500 dollars to remove the spell from Clarence. She insisted the spell she cast was much more difficult to remove.

After all the problems Clarence had been through recently, his parents were more than happy to pay for the wedding. Even though the girl he was marrying was not Creole, she was pretty. Though they felt he could have married better, they were more than happy that he was over that strange illness and that they would finally get a grandchild.

As Clarence raised the veil on her wedding dress to give Avonella the bridal salute, tears welled up in her eyes as she was happy for the first time ever in her life. *The things a girl has to do, to get her man,*she thought.

GUARDIAN (1982)

Levi Smith aka "Shine" was a product of the mean streets of Chicago. His Mother, Angie Thompson Smith, had roots in Thompsonville, Mississippi. She was a troubled youth who ran away to Chicago at age eighteen. She was married and pregnant before her twentieth birthday. Young Levi's father abandoned them before he was two years old and never took any responsibility for his son's upbringing.

Levi returned to Thompsonville to live with his grandmother after Angie's death from acute alcoholism. She succumbed before her thirty-eighth birthday. Thompsonville was Shine's home from age seventeen until he was twenty-two.

He never talked much about his life in Mississippi. These were not fond memories for him. He was raised in the big city and Thompsonville was always small potatoes and never a fit for him. When he moved to New Orleans, he settled in the Desire Projects which (during the times) was one of the toughest places to live in America.

He witnessed a violent act of murder his first week in Desire. "Sweet Willie" Taylor fatally stabbed Johnny Bourne because Johnny was seen going through the back door of Willie's apartment (on more than one occasion) while he was at work. Everybody knew Sweet Willie's "old lady" and Johnny had a thing for each other. Though Levi was already streetwise and tough, something about the violent act he witnessed triggered something dark inside him.

Levi "Shine" Smith built himself a reputation by demonstrating a cold and ruthless nature on more than one occasion. That reputation was necessary for his very survival.

Shine reached maturity at just over six feet. He had a smooth light brown skinned complexion and was quite handsome to the opposite sex, but, make no mistake, Shine Smith no longer had any emotional sensitivity towards the fairer sex. He possessed that certain air that even struck fear in younger, bigger and more powerfully built men. Most of the fear was because of reputation, but even those who didn't know him, instinctively knew he was a dangerous man.

After beginning his career as a professional, Shine became a loner. The only female companionship he had (or even wanted) was well financially compensated. He had been quite the ladies man when he arrived in New Orleans many years ago. He lived with Judy (the finest "Redbone" in Desire Projects) for two years before he hit his stride.

When they broke up, he got his first taste of independence and found he actually liked life better without strings. His loner trait perfectly complimented his chosen profession as a paid killer.

He was eccentric. Shine didn't do hard drugs. He could have also had a profitable career as a dealer but he despised junkies. He took special pleasure in dispatching them. On one occasion he *offed* two of them without contracts - just for his own personal satisfaction.

Shine was one of the city's premier hit men who had earned a lot of money for a long time working for the New Orleans gangs. The profession had always provided a very dependable living. Some young Turk, new to the organization, would always break the rules or step in the wrong direction and would have to be checked to set an example for the others. Shine was crafty and efficient and, most importantly, enjoyed his work.

He was now in his mid fifties and had made a small fortune in the business. He was well connected because of his relationships with the Uptown dealers. This meant he was also able to get plenty of work outside the gangs. He could have retired years ago, but still enjoyed the rush the job provided. He longed for that one last "hit" which would satisfy his craving and would be a fitting assignment to end his long career.

He routinely received packages with names, instructions, photos and cashier's checks at his post office box. This information was provided by Fast Frenchie, his sponsor.

Frenchie was a study in contrasts. He was the most powerful Black drug kingpin in New Orleans and probably the entire south. He was a handsome, very fair complexioned Creole who mixed comfortably on both sides of the color line.

Color was (and is still) an asset for a Negro in New Orleans. Frenchie was living proof skin color is mostly a visual phenomenon. Outside of New Orleans, he could pass for White and did so when it was to his advantage. He could also be Black as Black when that suited his purpose.

Shine didn't like working with the young bloods (as he referred to them), but he had worked with Frenchie for quite some time. Frenchie had always been fair with him even though fairness is never a real value to someone like Shine. Those in Shine's profession only respect ruthlessness and strength.

Shine's mind drifted back to his first job. That was at least thirty years ago. His mark was a slick pimp from Detroit who didn't know or chose to ignore the rules of property ownership in Uptown, New Orleans. He had tried to deal his wares in the wrong area and crossed the wrong people. Shine stalked him ten blocks down Canal Street before cornering him in an alley where he had gone to relieve himself. He was unaware he was being followed.

Shine stabbed him twenty times. The look of simultaneous fear and surprise on the pimp's face excited him. The control he felt and the violence of the act gave him a rush he hadn't felt since. After taking a bath and disposing of his bloody clothes, he slept extremely well that night. He knew he had found his calling.

It was another typical summer day in New Orleans. Shine lived in a nice flat in the French Quarters. He was starting to get edgy. He loved his work. His work was an addiction, and long periods between jobs gave him withdrawal. At times like this, he was doubtful he could retire under any circumstances.

He decided to walk through the quarter down to his box to see if any work had come in. Recent weeks had been somewhat of a slow period. Shine hadn't gotten a job since early May. It was now late June. The air was muggy which signaled the seasonal cycle of afternoon thunderstorms had begun in New Orleans.

Fast Frenchie, nee Ernest Antoine Boudreaux, sat comfortably in the large leather chair in his modern New Orleans East office. He took great pains to maintain his image as a hard working legitimate businessman. His Italian sponsor had coached him on how to maintain the proper image to protect himself from suspicion and arrest. Though few honest people knew his real business, he kept friends in high places and stayed deep enough in politics to keep himself immune from attack by overzealous officials.

Frenchie did the things necessary to be atop the heap in the city. He was shrewd. He didn't fear many people. Those that he did, were in some way, in his debt or his employ. Shine was both. He didn't truly fear Shine but he knew Shine was a man who liked his work a little too much to suit his tastes. Shine was an *old schooler* who had been around for a bit.

Frenchie had heard stories about him when he was a kid. Sometimes you had to take out someone, and a good hit man was a necessary professional Frenchie needed on his staff. He knew the difference between himself and Shine was that he had some kind of a conscience. Though he was in the illegal drug business and indirectly killed people every day, it was not quite the same as putting a gun to someone's head and pulling the trigger.

The phone rang. It was Eileen, his secretary. "It's Ronnie Leclaire."

Frenchie knew this was a call he had to take. Ronnie was the up and coming, *Mr. Big* in Gumbo City. "Hi, Ronnie. I got your package. I've made the necessary arrangements." That wasn't yet true, but Frenchie knew he had no choice in the matter.

"Well, I hope so," said LeClaire. "My contacts in Mississippi are anxious to get their project going and it can't go until the work I've given you has been completed."

One thing Frenchie hated was accepting responsibility for someone else's problems, but just as he was Shine's connection, LeClaire was his. These were the dues he paid for doing business as a man of color in the crescent city. They were minor dues by comparison to some other tasks he had to perform to get to his present position.

There was some property in nearby Mississippi that a group of White businessmen had been trying to acquire for some time. They had plans for a large casino and golf resort but most of the land they wanted belonged to that all-black town

Thompsonville, as he remembered.

"My contact told me those damn coons turned down a very generous offer," Ronnie said. "They ain't gonna go no higher; they want that "f...ing" property. I hope you're using your best guy on this one."

Frenchie knew he meant Shine. LeClaire knew of Shine though they had never met. The reason Frenchie had not yet acted was that he had some consternation regarding this hit. He couldn't say no because LeClaire was his sponsor, but he had a gut feeling about this one. Something about it left him just a little uneasy. Frenchie, like most New Orleanians, lived his life by feel. "Feel" had saved his life on more than one occasion growing up in New Orleans. Those were probably just hard-working Black people up in Mississippi minding their own business and trouble had come and sat right at their door - big trouble.

Thompsonville was located across the Mississippi state line about two hours north of New Orleans. It was slightly off the beaten path but was fast becoming a major commerce center in the southeastern part of the state. Nathaniel Thompson was the sixth Mayor of Thompsonville, Mississippi. He was cast in the mold of those who had preceded him. He was a visionary. He was serving his second term and had been re-elected unopposed. Nathaniel was forty-four, still physically fit though slightly gray with very thick hair. He was the father of two boys and a girl. Nathaniel married Nancy Campbell, his childhood sweetheart.

He finished Ole Miss Law school and set up his practice in Jackson. He worked very successfully there for seven years and amassed a nest egg before returning home to Thompsonville. The city had grown a bit since he left and was now able to support more lawyers. With Nancy and the kids' consent they returned home to Thompsonville. Marriage and life had been good for them in there. Nancy was his most ardent supporter and had inspired him to run for political office.

Nate Jr. and Elmer were now in college at Mississippi State. Bess was a sophomore at THS (Thompsonville High School). Nathaniel had promised his sons, he would make their basketball game in Starkville against Georgia on Saturday. Right now, that looked doubtful.

The Thompsonville population had doubled since Nathaniel was a kid. There was now about fifteen thousand residents in the town with another five thousand in the surrounding rural communities.

Nathaniel Thompson was a natural leader. He relished leading his hometown into the next millennium. This town, which represented so much to so many, was progressive yet still maintained the family atmosphere it had since he and Nancy were kids. For some reason, drugs and violence had not sucked the spirit of this community like they had many cities and towns in America.

As he gazed out the window of his office, he saw a steady stream of traffic moving on First Street. Thompsonville was an achievement for Blacks everywhere. Its land had been claimed and defended by ex-slaves during a time when survival was their only goal. Since then generations had survived and this town had flourished, and its sons and daughters had made great contributions to the state, the nation and the world.

"This is a very generous offer," stated Mark Johnson. "We can rebuild our park and put the new school out at Givens Lake. I believe a world class resort can put our community on the map." This was the bi-monthly meeting of the Thompsonville City Council. Nathaniel knew this issue wasn't dead, but he certainly hadn't expected Mark to rehash it.

"We've had our vote on this issue Mark and if we vote again, the result will be the same." The council had voted in March to reject the offer to sell city owned land to the Trinity Group of Brewton. The majority sentiment was that the community was not interested in changing its image after one hundred and eight years. As Marie Jackson had said when it was first presented, "Thompsonville represents progress, family, Christian values and hope for Black folks. Who knows what it will represent if we sell our heritage for their forty pieces of silver."

Mark was a transplant from up north and a progressive man. He commanded much respect on the council. There was a split on this issue when it was initially presented. Nathaniel had broken the tie with his vote. This spirit of a contrary opinion was welcomed in Thompsonville but Nathaniel and some others felt there was possibly something a little shady about the deal presented by the so called Trinity Group of Brewton. Thompsonville's relationship with its neighboring community had always been less than stellar.

"This is old business that we've already discussed, evaluated and voted on, let's not waste anymore of our time on this," said Arliss McCrae, the venerable member of the Thompsonville City Council.

With that comment, the discussion ended and went to new business. Nathaniel thanked Arliss (with just a visible nod and eye contact between them) for voicing his opinion on this issue. Arliss was well respected and was the official Thompson Bayou "Griot." Arliss had been best friends with Nate's father and had acted as his mentor after his father passed. He was very pleased to see Nathaniel return to Thompsonville, and be elected Mayor.

Shine received the contract information when he went to check his box on Thursday. Frenchie called Thursday night, "Listen Smith. I want to accompany you on this one." Shine listened silently and responded, "Now you know I don't work like that," he said.

"This is outside of the city and I think you need some insurance to close this deal," Frenchie responded.

This must really be an important hit if Frenchie was wanting to tag along. "I've done jobs outside of the city before. What's the big deal?" Shine shot back.

"I just have a hunch about this one," said Frenchie.

After a pause Shine remarked in a cold tone. "You always had a bitch streak in you."

The phone line was silent. Levi "Shine" Smith was the only Black man in New Orleans who had ever talked to Frenchie that way and lived. For two reasons - he only did it when he knew Frenchie needed him and he would never brag about doing it. Frenchie also knew this old Negro was really crazy and he didn't want to have to take out a first class "contractor" over something as silly as a disrespectful comment - not now anyway.

If he had made a comment like that with the wrong people present (people in his employ or his competitors or even LeClaire) street respect would demand a killing. He knew that and Shine knew that also.

"I'm concerned that this job goes off clean. It's very important to Mr. Big," stated Frenchie. He let Shine's comment pass, but realized the time could possibly come when he would have to take him out himself. He felt prepared to do so. He didn't get where he was by backing off of a challenge. "Thompsonville is that all-black town up in Mississippi. Folks say strange happenings go on up there at times. I don't believe it's going to be as easy to do this job as you may think."

Shine listened intently to Frenchie's assessment. He now recognized this as the assignment he had been waiting for. The horrific events of his youth seemed to be eons ago, but he knew this would be the job to end all jobs. He would complete it, without interference from Frenchie, and go away and enjoy the rest of his life. When Shine, AKA "Levi Smith", boarded that bus thirty years ago, leaving Thompsonville, he had a bitter taste in his mouth for the town and everything it represented. He hadn't been there since but he was looking forward to going back one more time. At last, he would have the opportunity to exorcise some of the demons of his youth.

"Look French," he was calmer now. "If you didn't know, I spent some time in that one-horse town of Thompsonville. I've got a score to settle. Besides, you don't have to worry. You know I always handle my business."

Thompsonville wasn't a place that held fond memories for him. He couldn't remember much about why he felt that way about his mother's hometown. He had always felt like an outcast there. He remembered spending two years of his time there in and out of reform school. His mind always seemed to black out the memory of the particular events that gave him such discomfort. "I don't think there's anything to worry about. This guy won't be a problem. I will be in and out of there in one night." For any other assignment Shine was probably totally correct, thought Frenchie.

"Okay Shine. Read this guy's bio one more time anyway. He's a very influential person. You need to cover your trail very well after this hit or it could come back to haunt all of us, (including LeClaire, thought Frenchie). Now think about that before you start this one."

Frenchie hung up the phone. That was his way of maintaining his position of authority. This was a necessary tactic. He knew Smith would see the light and come back to him with the right answer regarding this issue.

It was a rainy morning in Thompsonville. Nancy Campbell Thompson was a petite middle aged slightly graying woman who still retained quite a bit of her youthful figure and beauty. She clutched her solar plexus. There it was again. That uneasy feeling that always preceded trouble. It had been very uncomfortable for the past two days. She had mentioned it to her husband Nathaniel, last night. Nate always took his wife's premonitions seriously. She had *talent* as it was quietly referred to around here.

"How you feeling this morning, Honey," he asked as he kissed her good morning and took his juice from the counter.

"Hi Baby. I still feel uneasy. I can't yet tell what the source of this is, but I know you need to be careful," she stated with a loving look on her face.

This had been the only woman Nathaniel had ever desired since their marriage. He knew their kind of relationship was rare. It had been built on trust. He trusted her instincts. They had never been wrong. "Okay, Honey, I'll be careful, call me if you get more. Love you," he stated as he headed out the door.

Shine reluctantly agreed to let Frenchie accompany him to Thompsonville. They rode quietly up the interstate towards

Mississippi in the big black rental sedan. Frenchie leafed through the bio of one Nathaniel Terrell Thompson, Mayor of Thompsonville.

Frenchie stopped by Madam Lou's just yesterday. Madam Lou was his personal spiritual advisor. Every native of New Orleans in the *life* has one. She was, far and away, one of the most respected people in her profession in the city.

Frenchie had gone to her for years and she had never led him wrong. She had *the sight.* He almost always heeded her advice. Frenchie believed his connection to Madam Lou was a major key to his success. She was his trump card. She had always warned him when danger was lurking. Just having that insight ensured his longevity. She had told him on more than one occasion to beware of *the scorpion he* used to get ahead in his business. Thus, he was constantly aware of Smith. He always wore his bullet proof vest and he always carried his nine-millimeter and gun permit with him.

He was a sharp dresser and even attired in his protective undergarment the weapon was all but unnoticeable to any except those with trained eyes.

Madam Lou had said there was a veil she couldn't penetrate right now when she looked into his (Frenchie's) future. She indicated this happened at times and it meant he should be especially careful. What she didn't say was that there was some powerful magic blocking her vision today. Although she was a leading psychic and advisor in New Orleans, she was also a businessperson who didn't want to lose one of her best customers. Of course, though she did not share all of this information with Frenchie, her admonition to be careful should be good enough.

"How many more miles?" he asked Shine.

"We have about twenty more minutes," he responded. Shine hated to bring this young blood along. He often wondered how Frenchie was able to operate and control the largest drug empire in New Orleans for so long. There were smarter, more ruthless dealers in this city, but none had been able to successfully unseat this guy. He never could understand that.

Shine thought, if Frenchie didn't provide him such a good living, he would have taken him out himself (for a price), and that vest he wore when he was scared or the nine millimeter he always carried wouldn't help him a damned bit. A wry smile creased his lips as the thought of greasing Frenchie passed through his mind.

It was almost dusk as the big rental sedan entered the Thompsonville city limits. Though both men were fair complexioned, they didn't look out of place or suspicious at all as a police cruiser passed them in the left lane on state highway twenty seven.

Nancy felt a sensation so strong that she dropped a glass and the sound of it shattering on the tiled kitchen floor shocked her back to reality. She knew that the source of her discomfort was upon them. Thompsonville had never had bodyguards for its officials. That was just not a typical need in small town America. The talk was, the spirit of Dora Jane, the slave mother who provided the land where the town now stood, constantly watched over it and would never let any tragedy befall her kin.

As Nathaniel walked down the steps to his car, he paid no attention to the big sedan parked across the intersection near First Street. His drive home was only ten minutes, even in traffic. Nate didn't notice the sedan in his wake as he turned onto Dora Jane Road. Their home was located on the outskirts of Thompsonville.

As he pulled into the Fast Mart convenience store, Frenchie pulled up to the curb along seventh street. This would be an easier hit than he thought. Frenchie's palms were sweating. Even though he couldn't shake the feeling, he still had extreme confidence in Smith. Shine could feel Frenchie's nervousness as Nathaniel got out of his car and went inside the store. Frenchie's sense of foreboding was very strong. Frenchie somehow knew this wasn't the right time, even though he knew Smith was anxious to complete his task.

Much of life seems to be coincidental, however, the events that transpired over the seven minutes as Nathaniel exited the Seventh Street Fast Mart are amazing and are part of the

mystique of Thompsonville. If someone had recognized and brought attention to these occurrences, the Thompsonville legend would be even greater.

Shine had superstitions like anyone else, although he never wanted to admit them. He was jolted by the memory of his encounter with the Brewton Klansmen. He remembered Annie Sue. Sweet Annie Sue. He wondered if she was still around. He also remembered Chief Harvey Johnson and Russell Thompson. As he remembered the events of his last night in Thompsonville, it gave him a tinge of nerves. It was so long ago, and he had made peace with those strange events that saw his life take a different turn.

After reading a target's bio, Shine would make the decision to kill at close range or from a distance. This decision was based on some deep subconscious evaluation of the character of the person. Pimps and gang people, he almost always killed at close range, looking them squarely in the eye. He fed off of their fear and emotion. He killed innocents from a distance. Innocents were people who were not in the business; or their involvement in it could not be ascertained. On this basis, Nathaniel was designated as a distance kill. The weapon Shine chose was an automatic rifle with a silencer. Shine was an excellent marksman. He had practiced with this particular gun for a week and was now able to put twenty out of twenty rounds in the bulls eye with the silencer at thirty yards. The rifle was acquired for this special purpose. It was untraceable. Its serial number had been filed off. Shine would perform the deed, remove the silencer and drop the rifle at the scene of the killing.

Thompsonville, and what it stood for meant nothing to him.

As an icon of the black struggle, it meant only slightly more to Frenchie. Business was business. Frenchie's loyalty was only to his pockets.

A steady drizzle was a perfect mask for the dark deed about to be performed. Nathaniel's car was the only vehicle outside the convenience store when he entered. He stayed inside the store exactly six minutes. During that time, other cars drove up and patrons went inside. Frenchie was the lookout and became even more uncomfortable as other cars started to drive up. He had extreme confidence in Smith's ability to cleanly ice this guy, but there was still that nagging discomfort in the pit of his gut. Suddenly Frenchie felt a strange fear for himself that he hadn't felt since he was a young man growing up in the ninth ward.

His first fight had forged the direction of his life. Frenchie was picked on because of his light skin. In the neighborhood where he grew up, you either had to fight or take plenty of ass-whippins if your complexion was too light. He demonstrated his ability to street fight after first tasting his own blood. He cold cocked Jamie Felton with a brick. Bam!! The fight was over. He thought, at first, he had killed him, but Jamie regained consciousness and though he was a little older than Frenchie, he nor any of the neighborhood *toughs,* ever messed with Frenchie again. Jamie was a little "off" after he bashed him with the brick. Though Frenchie's fear through that encounter was transformed into brazenness, he certainly did not feel that particular emotion right now.

Frenchie regained his composure somewhat and convinced himself the two of them could handle this job (even if it got messy). He knew how important this was to LeClaire which is why he designated himself as the insurance.

Shine positioned himself behind a tree in the vacant lot next to the store. He couldn't be seen by anyone driving down the street. Even though Frenchie's palms had stopped sweating, he still didn't feel in control of this situation. He had wanted to tell Smith to scrub this for now and try to get the mark at his home or somewhere else.

Shine was set and ready. He would pull the trigger twice, Thompson would fall and nobody would even realize he had been shot. During that time, he and Frenchie would slowly drive out of town. They would switch cars at the first rest stop on interstate fifty-nine and be back in New Orleans before midnight.

But, as has always been said, "the best laid plans of mice and men," was the case for Levi Smith and Earnest Antoine Boudreaux.

In spite of the activity, as Nathaniel Thompson exited the store, Smith got off the perfect shot. Then a strange sequence of events began. Nathaniel had his change, seven cents, in his right hand. While exiting the store he accidentally dropped the coins and immediately bent down to retrieve them. The shot from the rifle, which would have snuffed out his life in that split second, instead went six inches over his head. It hit Sammy Stevens, who was directly behind Nathaniel, in his left shoulder. Sammy screamed aloud as blood and bone fragments splattered other customers standing behind him in the store.

Shine was completely outdone. He had never had such a freak thing happen to him. Frenchie, able to see what had happened, was beside himself beckoning Shine to get in the car. As Nathaniel stood up amid the confusion, Shine had the presence of mind to squeeze off another shot. This was meant to be a head shot. Because of his disappointment with his first shot he clearly missed the second shot by two inches; just that tiny lapse in concentration by Shine, saved Nathaniel's life a second time. For an expert marksman like Shine, two inches is a mile. This, again, had never happened to him before.

Nathaniel heard the whizz and felt the heat of the bullet as it passed over his head. He heard the dull thud of the silencer and the bullet fragments break a jar of vinegar on a shelf in the store. He turned to see what had happened to Sammy.

"Someone's shooting!" yelled another store patron. Everyone in the store dropped to the floor. Miles Cooley, the store manager pressed the silent alarm and police cruisers were rolling towards the Seventh Street Fast Mart. Car seventy-seven which, was less than two blocks away, made a u-turn and proceeded to the scene. In anger and frustration, Shine got off three more rounds that broke more merchandise in the store. These shots also missed the target. He then headed back to the rental car. He was beside himself with rage. This shouldn't be happening. Frenchie was waving to Shine to get in the car so they could leave.

Nancy Thompson was on the phone to the Thompsonville

police trying to track down Nathaniel's whereabouts. The tightness now felt like a fist in her solar plexus. She noticed the time was exactly 9:07pm. "We haven't had any accident reports at all Ms. Thompson," said the police dispatcher "but there is a silent alarm at the Fast Mart on Seventh Street." She knew Nathaniel sometimes stopped there to pick up things on his way home. She grabbed the keys to the truck and rushed out of the house heading to the Fast Mart.

By this time Nathaniel and everyone in the store knew there was a shooter. Sammy was still screaming on the floor in his own blood mixed with glass and the cold beer he had just purchased.

Frenchie was upset. The plan to drive slowly away from the scene was in jeopardy as cruisers with lights flashing were coming from both directions.

"Let's get out of here," said Shine as he entered the car on the passenger side.

This whole situation was starting to seem surreal. Shine always had clean hits. Frenchie was too smart to be caught in such compromising situations. Both men were feeling outdone by their own missteps. Shine could see Frenchie's displeasure. He lapsed into his street talk to betray his fear. "Just be cool, French," he said. "Drive slow, jus' look like we had nothin' to do with dis."

Frenchie was sweating bullets. It seemed as though someone or something was conspiring against them. The big sedan pulled slowly from the curb as people in the store were pointing in their direction. Two officers were walking towards the car with their revolvers unholstered. "Hey, you wait!" one yelled. About that time a black cat ran right across the path of the vehicle and Frenchie (already tense) floored the accelerator. The tires screeched loudly on the pavement as the vehicle roared up the avenue.

Two Thompsonville police cruisers were in hot pursuit when the sedan crossed Evans Street moving about eighty miles per hour. The car ran six of the seven lights on Dora Jane Highway on its way out of town.

"They're so close, we won't be able to lose them!" Frenchie complained. In fact, the police cars were gaining fast. An all points bulletin from the Thompsonville police to the Mississippi State Highway Patrol had them already setting up a roadblock at the interstate's *on* ramp. This location was about seven miles from Thompsonville's City Limits.

As Nancy Thompson arrived at the Fast Mart, the tension in her solar plexus was completely gone. Her husband Nathaniel was okay and was busy giving first aid to Sammy.

As they cruised down Highway 27 at one hundred seven miles per hour, all Frenchie could think about was going to state prison in Angola. He knew he wouldn't last a week. First, he was a light skinned Negro, but the greater issue was the lives that had been destroyed by the poison he sold. He had also sanctioned hits on relatives of many of those incarcerated there. He had many enemies and not enough friends there.

Shine didn't think about anything. The excitement of this crisis situation was having a strange effect on him. Premonition of death created a weird kind of excitement. To this point, it was always someone else's death. Tonight, it could be his own.

The sedan was traveling so fast, it couldn't make the sharp turn at Possum Tree Curve. Even without the rain slick pavement, a safe turn would have been impossible. The highway sign read, "Slow to 35 MPH." Many had failed to negotiate this turn at much lower speeds than the big sedan was traveling. The investigator estimated the vehicle was doing approximately ninety-seven miles per hour when it exploded through the guardrail. It was fully airborne for one hundred feet before coming to a sudden and complete stop at the base of a huge pine tree. The sudden stop spelled instantaneous death for the two vehicle occupants.

Al Smith, the Thompsonville police sergeant, reached down to pick up the vehicle's Louisiana license plate from the shoulder of the road. As he looked at his watch, it read 9:27pm on July 27th. Then, he saw the vehicle burst into violent flames. He would record this as the time of the accident and the death of the occupants of the vehicle in his report.

At that same time (9:27pm) at "La Louisianne" restaurant in

the French Quarter, Ronnie LeClaire was pronounced dead after six attempts by paramedics to shock his failed heart back to functionality proved unsuccessful. Ronnie was a good physical specimen. Though he was a gangster, he was one of the new breed, (healthy, respectable and clean living). He was a jogger and a tennis player and didn't drink very much (perhaps a little wine). He was right in the middle of his favorite ethnic joke when he suddenly turned beet red and slumped face forward into his seafood pasta.

Indeed, residents of Thompsonville, and the children of Dora Jane seemed to have a guardian watching over them. Tragedy was averted by inexplicable events. Ronnie LeClaire had been the Louisiana syndicate's champion for the Trinity Group's Casino and Golf Course project in Mississippi. The strange circumstances of his death took focus away from that project. Syndicate members were busy for quite some time trying to figure out who put the hit out on Ronnie and how.

After the events of July 27th, the Big Easy would rest even easier until new kingpins began to assert themselves to claim newly abandoned drug territories.

If the successors to Fast Frenchie or Ronnie LeClaire retained the services of Madam Lou, she surely would have issued the admonition, "If longevity is your desire, steer clear of Thompsonville."

THE NEW AGE NEGRO
Self Realization
(1989)

Though the sun shone above his head in terms of his life's progression, things were now moving fast for William Thompson. To be sure, he was still a young man and he had enjoyed financial success, however, his life's true mission was yet to be revealed. His education in the sciences and finance had brought his career far. Prosperity had come his way early and with that came the freedom to choose. Choices were still a luxury for most Black men. It was now time for Will Thompson to again make a major change in his life.

His older Cousin Russell was his mentor and confidant as a young man growing up in Thompsonville. Although William had decent athletic ability, he didn't concentrate on sports in high school. He was always the serious student, though he was by no means a saint. He certainly found his share of the usual mischief with his friends growing up in rural Mississippi. He graduated at the top of his class at Thompsonville High and received a full academic scholarship to Tuskegee Institute.

Will's financial success began with the two inventions he patented while a sophomore engineering student at Tuskegee. One was a special hydraulic coupling which he sold to a large Aerospace engineering firm for an amount which equaled a king's ransom for a young Black man. This was unprecedented for a college student during these times. Will's Cousin Russell personally brokered the patent sale and insured young William's sale proceeds were invested wisely. This was no easy task for any Negro to accomplish but, Will knew, with Russell negotiating on his behalf, he had a distinct advantage. He was extremely appreciative of Cousin Russell's help.

Though brilliant in the field, William Thompson knew engineering would probably not be his life's calling. After graduate school, he changed career directions and went to work for a financial consulting firm in New York. He interned his first year as a financial analyst. After his internship, he enjoyed moderate career success and added much to his financial nest egg.

After many years in New York, Will never felt quite in tune with the city. His childhood and the events which molded him seemed like a million years ago.

William was offered many positions with large engineering firms after completing his undergraduate work. He didn't consider any of those. Instead, he had moved to New York after graduating Tuskegee to complete his master's in business at NYU. Even the best of the Negro engineering graduates were only offered positions as technicians or less. Though he had two patents in his own name by the time he finished his undergraduate studies, he got no offers to work as an engineer, associate engineer or even junior engineer. William Thompson made a personal vow to never sell himself for less than what he perceived his value to be. He chose not to work for any company for less money or prestige than he felt he was worth. This vow made a career path change a necessity.

New York City and a career in finance provided little time to slow down and contemplate the more serious aspects of his life. The years passed quickly. After his personal tragedy, Will was consumed with education. He became a man on a mission. He endured the challenges presented to him as Cousin Russell said he would. Education was indeed the means to his end. His older brothers had successful careers and provided necessary financial comfort for his mother and father. As the youngest child, he felt no great pressure from family to excel, but he was personally motivated from inside himself to answer his calling.

His personal need for spiritual self-realization was now the primary driver in his life. Though he spent much time studying to support his career in finance, Will was a seeker of esoteric knowledge. This particular pursuit moved social relationships to the fringes of the circle he lived in.

He played Y basketball and played golf in a regular work foursome. Something about the mathematics involved in the game of golf intrigued him. Thompsonville (the little town he grew up in) to this day did not have a single golf course. He had learned the game as an undergraduate freshman and had been good enough to be the alternate on the college golf team in his first year. His fellow team members were amazed that he never even touched a golf club before he came to Tuskegee but he was a natural. As a college player, he achieved all he wanted to accomplish in that sport. He was ranked number two player on the men's golf team his senior year.

These many years after college, sports were now just activity mechanisms that kept him physically healthy and allowed him to release the pressures of his work. In spite of personal accomplishments, he fought the single enemy of loneliness.

He and Rosita had been serious in high school. She was the first girl he ever kissed. Sure, there were prettier girls, but, in his eyes, none were as pretty as she was. For William Thompson, she was all he could ever want (looks, personality and character). After all these years, he could still remember her soft lips. Though they had never been intimate, she had truly been his soul mate. They had both vowed to wait until their wedding night to fully consummate their relationship. They had eyes for each other since they were both in grade school. Though now a man of forty three, these faint memories were still burned somewhere deeply in his heart.

Will had unceremoniously lost his virginity in graduate school. A female professor at NYU had blatantly seduced him. The physical act provided no real meaning for him at the time. All he could think of during the act was what it would have been like with the true love of his life, Rosita. Through his years in New York, he had one or two semi-meaningful relationships, but none serious enough to contemplate marriage. In the back of his mind, he was even now beginning to doubt his sexuality.

He was a handsome and financially successful man. His entire package was very attractive to the opposite sex, but recent relationships never provided that spark to ignite that special something in a relationship.

Rosita's passing was the most tragic thing that had ever happened in his life. Cousin Russell tried to help him put that event into perspective. "Son, you can't change what must be. None of us can. You must remember life is the road we must all travel (kings, queens, paupers and slaves). Some of us have longer journeys. Some have just a single stop. I believe true love has a deeper meaning that extends beyond this journey we are all making. What you and Rosita had will always exist. Though her time may be over, yours continues. You'll meet another special someone and the relationship you'll have with that person will be richer because of what you and Rosita had."

Those words didn't quite reach Will's heart, even years after her untimely departure. Russell was, of course, always right. Mary Rosita Anderson and her friend Annie Smith were victims of a hit and run driver on Main Street in Thompsonville walking home after a Thompsonville High School basketball game. She was a high school senior and this happened during Will's freshman year at Tuskegee.

Will was so despondent he considered dropping out of school and enlisting in the Army. Russell convinced him Tuskegee was where he needed to be. That is what Rosita would want for him. According to Russell, she was probably still looking after him and supporting his every effort. He reluctantly went back to college and rededicated himself to his studies in an effort to overcome the pain of his loss.

It would be years before the sadness would lift itself from his heart. It was now the nineteen eighties. The Black man had found a different place in these times. Blacks in America had years ago discovered pride in their identity. As Blacks were now becoming integrated into the social and economic fabric of American society, they were beginning to enjoy some of that which Will and the other residents of Thompsonville had always had. Cousin Russell and others in Thompsonville had secretly and not so secretly provided that special something that made Thompsonville the unique town it was.

Will knew in his heart what Russell and some others provided for Thompsonville would in some form also be his personal heritage. Though he began developing his talent in grade school, over the years he had pushed his talent into the shadows. His only experience since childhood had been his strong premonition of Rosita's death.

He was so overcome with anxiety on the day she died, he was unable to attend classes. He spoke with her just minutes before she left home for the game, but even then he was unable to touch the source of his anxiety and agitation. He still remembered Rosita's soft voice and bright eyes. Her easy smile and sense of humor was a rare quality. Her presence gave him a peace his heart had yet to know with anyone else. She had an uplifting spirit that always saw the positives in every situation. She was indeed the *yin* his *yang* required. They were so attuned he could tell when she came into the room without even looking up. The sound of her peculiar footfalls resonated in his heart. Will shook himself from his reverie.

He had plenty to do this week. He reviewed his accounts. He had achieved the financial goals, three times over what he set for himself fifteen years earlier. This was the only company he had ever worked for. He had progressed to Department Head during his time there, although his skill and ability probably warranted more. Certainly, lesser skilled employees, who began their careers after Will, had already made vice president.

Will signed his resignation letter, put in an envelope and deposited it in the inter-company mail. Chad Stewart, his Vice President, would be disappointed, but Will knew it was time. With the money he had saved and invested, he would never have to work again and would still be able to live a very comfortable life well beyond normal retirement age. He had also recently sold his apartment Uptown which turned a handsome profit.

He was no longer preoccupied with making money. He personally had no great love for it. It only represented freedom to find real meaning in his life. Now was the time to change directions in an effort to find his true mission.

Russell said, "Everyone has one. It's up to that person to recognize what it is and accomplish it."

"You know a lot of things Russell. What is my life mission?" William one day asked his older cousin.

"If I knew I wouldn't tell you," he said. It would be against all spiritual rules to tell someone that kind of information. Besides, growth is gained in the process of finding out for yourself."

Will had already said most of his good-byes. He looked at his plane ticket to Phoenix. The van lines had picked up his belongings last Friday and he had moved to the Somerset Hotel where he would stay for the next week until he departed on Saturday morning. The nice adobe he purchased in Sedona had a magnificent view and would provide him the solitude he would need to work on those things he felt the need to accomplish.

It was as if an alarm clock inside him had gone off. Things had been tough during the past three months. His routine was completely broken. He couldn't sleep or eat much at all. He found himself up at two am each night staring at the four walls of his bedroom. He started the practice of meditating again. He hadn't done that since he was in high school. He would light a candle, empty his mind of all thought and sit in the lotus position for an hour or more.

This process gave him clarity and mental energy he hadn't felt since he was a child. His psychic ability was returning.

This in itself made it almost impossible to work in his

current job any longer. The noise and disjointed energy in the workplace was very discomforting to him. He was *sensitive.* He could read and feel others' thoughts and emotions, but he would never use this information for personal gain. He could also see certain aspects of their past and future. This was very disconcerting. He knew of his ability long ago. He absolutely had to shut this down for awhile to accomplish the goals he set for himself for college and beyond. He knew in shutting down this ability, it would come back one day at a time in which he would have no control. He would have to just ride the wave.

This was one of the aspects of his relationship with Rosita. She, along with Cousin Russell, was one of those quiet people that he received no extra sensory feedback from. She was a person who was quiet mentally to him. Russell believed that those with pure intentions and hearts were made that way. This is one of the reasons Will was somewhat standoffish in establishing relationships. He could imagine meeting, falling in love with and marrying someone and having his psychic ability come back with a vengeance. Then he'd find out that person wasn't really in love with him at all but married him for convenience or other reasons. Worse yet, he would find other things about that person he didn't want to know.

Will was a man of forty-three years who was yet to fulfill his life's calling. It was now time for the chickens to come home to roost. His present situation no longer would allow that.

He was moving to a place that would later become a "New Age" Mecca for those on the spiritual path. He would seek his life direction in Sedona, Arizona.

He spent a week in Sedona ten years before he decided to move there. He had never been to a more beautiful place. Its red rocks and its spiritual vortexes gave him a peace he had never felt anywhere else. He felt at one with the area and the magic that emanated from it.

"How much will that be?" The slightly gray haired man asked.

"Please put any donation you would care to leave in the jar on the table," Will replied.

"They said you were good," the smallish middle-aged woman who accompanied the man to Will's shop said.

He was fully transitioned from his previous career and now gave life readings in his small shop on the outskirts of Sedona. He gained great satisfaction from helping others. He was only open three days a week from ten to two. Business had still been pretty brisk of late. The jar on the table was almost filled to the top with singles, fives, tens, twenties and even a few hundreds and some coins. He would drive down to Phoenix on Fridays and make a contribution to the Main Street Mission.

He felt extreme satisfaction for what he gave to those who sought him out. Some were just curious about a Black man in this part of the country who did what he did. Others were legitimately in search of the best in his profession. Those rare few were on their spiritual quest. He got special satisfaction in helping guide these people to the proper path. He smiled inwardly at being able to help others while he was still a seeker himself.

Will became an active member in Sedona's growing *new age* community. He walked the Sedona trails and meditated at many of its spiritual power places during sunset. He joined a meditation group shortly after relocating there. It was regularly held at one of the group members' homes. A large number of the community attended this meditation group. He looked forward to tonight's meeting. As a spiritual seeker, he felt the need to establish himself as a viable member of this group.

Will was now forty-four. Though his life mission was starting to become clear, he was still yet to meet that special someone who intrigued him until tonight. There were fifteen people in the room. Will knew most of them with the exception being a petite brown-haired woman. She was very attractive to him, yet he could see she was no more than early twenties. Most of the group were older - late thirties and above. Most were those on the spiritual path. As Will's power came back, he instinctively knew most things about any person he met. Will observed from across the room that the young lady was looking his way. He could not discern her racial makeup. He sensed one thing that got his extreme attention. She was mentally silent. Nobody else in the gathering was.

He would have to meet her and dialog with her to be sure.

During their meditation exercises the entire group became almost mentally silent. Will would approach her when the session was complete.

The gentle touch of the hand on his left shoulder surprised him. He turned to see the most beautiful smile he had seen in more than twenty years. "I'm Dorinda and you're thee William Thompson," she said.

For the first time in a long time he was caught off guard. "You remind me of someone. Have we met before?" He asked.

"I don't think so. I've heard a lot about you though," she remarked.

"You're so young to travel in a circle such as this," he stated. "I'm not as young as I look. My mother says I'm an old soul. I've always been interested in things such as this."

Will observed her mannerisms. Her comfort and sense of familiarity with him was almost overpowering. He hadn't felt the stirrings he was having now in a long time. He felt like he did the first time he and Rosita took a walk together and talked under the oak tree after church. He felt those same school boy sensations he had so many years ago. His sweating palms and nervous knees in this situation were an enigma to him. They conversed for a full half-hour until the host came and took Dorinda to meet another of the regular attendees. He observed her walk. He had only seen one other woman walk that way. Could it be? He knew in providing readings for others that many believed past lives were a strong possibility. Could she be who he thought she was? As he began to realize his psychic and clairvoyant skill, he knew an open mind was invaluable.

He and Dorinda found time and reason to spend much time together over the next few weeks. A walk here or a lunch there. He found out she was twenty-four. She was from Sacramento, California. She was multiracial. She had already completed her master's degree in psychology at Arizona State. She had taken a year off after graduate school to write a book. She chose to spend her year in Sedona. She still wasn't sure why she picked Sedona over Maui but even that was becoming clearer for her.

They both believed in "flow" (he spiritual cause and effect and its relationship to circumstances and outcomes). In life there are no coincidences. Everything happens for a reason. Dorinda was so much more mature than her years. She was the most interesting woman he had met since his childhood sweetheart.

The days passed swiftly since they met that night. Will knew the time was near when they would probably consummate their relationship. He was excited and apprehensive at the same time.

He called Cousin Russell one night to talk about the issue of his relationship with Dorinda. "Will, you know as well as I do this is an area in which I probably can't help you much. Except in rare circumstances, I have a blind spot towards you just like you probably have for me. You're on your own on this one. I have faith in you. You've made good decisions all your life. I'm sure you'll make the right one in this situation."

The encouragement Russell provided settled him emotionally and gave him confidence. It was January 26th. This day would have marked Rosita's forty third birthday. It was also Dorinda's twenty-fifth birthday and was a special occasion for them both. They spent a quiet evening at his adobe. He demonstrated his fine culinary skills as they dined on grilled salmon and shared a bottle of white wine.

After finishing the wine, they retired to the bedroom. She was as beautiful with her clothes off as she was with them on. Will, though nineteen years her senior, was very fit for a man over forty. Their bodies glistened in the moonlight which shone through the bedroom window. As they embraced and explored each other, time stood still. As his lips found hers the rhythmic passion of their lovemaking moved to a crescendo. It had never been like this with anyone else for Will. He hadn't been sexually active in a long time, and Dorinda didn't have much experience, but their deep feelings for each other made this the most enjoyable union either had ever known. After they finished making love, they spent time talking to one another about many things. They slept off and on and caught a glimpse of the sun rising as they completed their last passionate act.

As she slept, William rubbed his fingers across the small birthmark on the back of her neck. It looked like a small brown butterfly. It was identical to the one Rosita had in the same place on her neck. Tears welled in his eyes as he realized its significance. He softly whispered, "Welcome back. You've made me wait a long time."

TRAVELER (1978)

Regret is a useless emotion. As Andrew Miller looked into the mirror of his life, regret was all he could feel. The jagged scar that extended from the top of his head to the bottom of his right cheek was only what could be described as "hideous". It represented so much wasted potential. He felt pain every day and none of it was from the scar, the loss of his right eye or his limp.

Prior to the accident, Andrew's life had been pretty good. His future was bright. He was the fourth child in a family of three boys and four girls. He had always been the life of the house. He was a smart child and was (if not his Dad's) certainly his mother's favorite. He got along well with all of his siblings except his brother Eli. Eli was only one year younger, but felt it was his mission in life to keep Andrew's feet on the ground in all aspects of his life.

Andrew sometimes wished his dad had taken their family and moved up north during the great migration.

Thompsonville, for him, was just a one horse town and before the accident, he looked forward to living in the big city.

Before the accident, Andrew had a confident and almost arrogant air to his personality. Though the girls were crazy about his good looks and swagger, he didn't have any serious relationships.

He had managed to get himself a "taste of honey" on more than a few occasions, however, he played the field until he got to college. Secretly he was excited about one day, leaving Mississippi to pursue his fame and fortune in the big city.

His sisters and brothers each left Thompsonville after college graduation. They had all gone to southern Black colleges on scholarship, just as he did, before the accident. Dad and Mom stressed education. Though he was a decent student, he got somewhat of a pass because he was the town football star. Junior, Ellen and Lynette all were working and had good careers up north. Now even Eli had found his way to Los Angeles and had a good job working there. His younger sisters were both high school teachers in Dallas. In his mind, he was the only child in their family still left in backwoods Mississippi. Theirs was probably the only family in this mostly Black town that were not Thompsons or relatives of them. In spite of that fact, the Millers were accepted and very respected in the Thompsonville community. Dad and Mom had moved here from Natchez when they were both in their twenties.

This was the South of the late seventies and things were

changing for the Black man in the world, but (because of the accident) this was a ship that had left the dock without him. Andrew was now thirty one and worked as a mechanic at the town's Ford dealership. It was a respectable job, but not what he had envisioned as his future.

His personal loss from the accident was great. The long rehabilitation took so much from him. He was a star football player at Jackson State when the accident happened. The accident ended his football career and his college education. With his good looks and swagger gone, he became a recluse who would probably never again leave the town he was born in.

His mother yelled from the kitchen, "Andrew, Mr. Brock is on the phone." Mr. Brock was his supervisor at the dealership. He respected Andrew's work and treated him as well as any man could expect to be treated in the workplace.

When he came out of his room, his Mom Linda (as positive as ever) greeted him with hot breakfast and a smile. "Morning Honey, what did Mr. Brock want?" Linda was a great mom. That was a real blessing in his life. Andrew was the only child still at home and he felt he would probably be there until the end.

"He wanted to know if I could stay late tonight to complete the work on the transmission job we have for Ms. Winston."

"You know we have bible study tonight. You've missed two weeks in a row. Karen Smith asked about you last week." His mom had goals for him that he didn't even have for himself. He knew Karen (who was a very nice girl) liked him in spite of his injury, but his heart was so wounded, he had no desire to even entertain trying to live a normal life.

"I know Mom. I'm just so tired after work, all I can do some nights after a bath is to get in bed." His Mom smiled and patted his head affectionately as she placed his plate and milk glass on the table.

His first real girlfriend was Miss Jackson State, Rose Parker, who was a stunning beauty from Clarksdale. She was easily the best-looking girl on campus. Even Andrew, football hero and big man on campus, was proud to have her on his arm at student events.

She had never returned to see him after they removed the bandages from his face. The accident was also a real tragedy for the school. They lost three of their all-conference players and two All American candidates in that accident. One lost his life and two would never play the game again. The driver, Sammy Williams (the other All American candidate who died in the crash), was already being scouted by NFL teams. His continued success would have changed the fortunes of his family. Two of his brothers were in Parchman Prison. The last sibling was born with a birth defect and would never be able to take care of himself. The NFL signing bonus Sammy would have gone a long way toward changing the fortunes of his family.

Andrew not only felt hurt for himself, but also for Sammy and his family. The other passenger Evan "Swill" Thomas from Gulfport broke his leg in two places and would recover but would never again be a college football player. They were on their way to see Swill's younger brother (who was the quarterback for Gulfport High), played in the state championship game against Laurel. They were driving under the speed limit because of the wet roads, but were cut off by a speeding semi which caused the Chevy to lose traction and roll over five times before slamming into a large pine tree.

It still hurt to think about it. Swill did return to school to finish his education. He was now working in Detroit for one of the large automakers. Swill called from time to time, but Andrew never returned his calls. Jackson State also offered to honor the academic portion of Andrew's scholarship. He declined and chose instead to go to Thompsonville Vo-Tech. He finished the automotive engineering training program and worked at Thompsonville Ford since graduating.

The change was profound. "Why is it you don't do any of the things you used to do?" Eli asked. "Mama told me all you do is sit in your room or go to the library and read when you're not at work. Why don't come and spend some time here with me in California when you take your vacation?"

Though he and Eli were always competitive growing up, their relationship had taken a different turn after the accident. Eli had gone on to law school and now worked in Los Angeles. The competitive issues that were always between them were gone. Eli seemed to have nothing but pity for him, which left a pain in his heart that would not go away.

Three years after Andrew's accident, his father passed away

suddenly of a heart attack. It seemed sorrow was being heaped on in big piles. His Dad was a good man who provided well for his family. He was respected in the community, but kept his distance from Andrew even more after the accident. If Andrew had a regret, it was the fact that he and his father, Richard Miller (Big Rich), didn't have a closer relationship. Andrew knew that was mostly his fault. He also knew his dad was very proud of his sports accomplishments. Big Rich quietly bragged to his friends about Andrew's accomplishments on the football field and came to all of his high school games and most of his games in Jackson. His father was now gone and they would never enjoy the relationship a father was supposed to have with his sons.

The family gathered to support their mom with their dad's passing. She would never have to leave the family home. Between their contributions and the insurance, she was well taken care of.

Andrew had been very popular in high school and in college. His transition to recluse was hard to accept by both friends and family. In his heart, he felt he was no longer attractive to the opposite sex. His bravado and swagger was completely gone.

Andrew came to realize his physical wholeness and good looks had always defined who he was. Most of his high school buddies had all left Thompsonville to pursue careers in the cities. One or two remained, but he no longer had things in common with any of them.

He went to church periodically with his Mom and his sisters and brothers when they came home to visit. Even those infrequent visits did not give him comfort. Neither family nor church could heal the wound that was so deep in his heart.

He believed in the principles of the church he was raised in. Because of these principles, he knew taking his own life would not be an acceptable option to relieve his pain; however, he still struggled with this choice.

Linda had arranged for him to talk with Reverend Washington which had not gone well at all. He knew his mom had only his welfare in mind, but he was not convinced someone who had never walked in his shoes could tell him how to pull himself out of the hole he was in.

Work helped. He was absolutely one of the best transmission mechanics at Thompsonville Ford, but he had believed in his heart (prior the accident) he was destined for a different and greater future. He had envisioned a professional career and a family of sons and daughters, but that was all gone for him now. Who would want a "broken man"? If only things could be different. If he could only go back and change those things in the past that set his life on this tragic course, perhaps he would be living a much different life.

Andrew was an avid user of the Thompsonville Library. He did research on everything. He had once read a science fiction book on time travel. He read all he could on many subjects. A lot was gleaned from his library reading.

Time travel, he read, was just a pipe dream but one of the few things that could keep his mind off the solution he did not want to consider.

Most serious scientists considered time travel an impossibility. Einstein proved that time, theoretically slows down when one approached the speed of light. But Andrew didn't see how any of that applied to him going back in time to change his future. All of that weird thinking was causing his head to spin. Anyone who knew him would think him a fool for some of the thoughts he had in his head these days.

He didn’t do much for entertainment or socialization. He was a loner. There were a couple of guys with whom he drank an occasional beer after work. He sometimes went to the movies alone. For brief moments work, reading and movies took his mind off his personal misery. Surely if he couldn't find a way to revive his life, God wouldn’t begrudge him an early exit.

He had just finished watching a movie at the Ritz theatre when he noticed someone standing near him that he thought he recognized. It was an older gentleman. It was a cool October Mississippi Friday evening. The man approached him with a friendly greeting. “Hello Andrew,” he said. “How are you these days?”

It was Mr. Russell Thompson. He was well known around town. He was a man nobody spoke badly about, but Andrew (as always) didn’t want to be bothered with mundane conversation. “I’m fine Mr. Russell. How are you?”

Russell was a somewhat tall, graying man who appeared very fit for his age. His eyes were clear and his face was very smooth. To be sure he didn't know what Mr. Russell did, but he knew he was an important person in these parts. That was really saying something around here so he didn't just blow him off.

"On your way home? Let's stop at Mae's diner and let me buy you a coffee or a soda."

Andrew's smile turned serious as he looked at Russell who picked up the change and responded in-kind. "You've had a lot of weight on you, son, and you look like you could use a friend. I've been out of town for a couple weeks and I promised myself I would make time to see you when I got back to Thompsonville."

Andrew gave him a curious look and wondered what this was about. Mr. Russell had never spoken to him in his life. Even when he was an All-State high school football star, he was never one of those seeking his time or attention.

It was just a short walk to Mae's diner, and not much further home. "Sure Mr. Russell, what's this all about?" Andrew played on championship teams with Russell's cousins (Marlon and Michael Thompson). They were twins and both had received scholarships to play football at Grambling. Marlon went on to play professionally with the Kansas City Chiefs.

As they entered the diner, only two of the twelve tables were occupied.

"Sit wherever you like," Mae said as they entered.

As they sat down, Russell began a polite conversation. "Sometimes things in life look insurmountable" he started.

Andrew wondered to himself. *Who was this guy to think he knew how I felt and what I was thinking?*

"I knew your dad very well. I know how proud he was of you. He would be very disappointed right now."

Andrew took offense at this statement, but he still respected Mr. Russell and did not respond with an impolite reply.

Russell continued, "I sense you have given up and you feel life has nothing more to offer and you have nothing else to give the world. I beg to differ. You've taken your lumps and though I know you have not completely given up, I also know you're close."

Andrew squirmed in his chair as Russell spoke. He wanted to get up and leave, but something made him stay. The audacity this man displayed intrigued him. His dad and mom had tried to have a similar conversation with him a year after the accident, but he would hear none of it. He got up and walked out of the room and they never approached him again.

"How would you know what I'm thinking?" Andrew replied with a look of disgust.

Russell was completely unfazed by his response. He continued, "In crisis, there is opportunity. When you fall in life, even if you think you've been pushed, don't wallow.

Get up. Dust yourself off and keep moving. Most of all, be patient. None of us knows what the universe has in store for us." Russell could tell his words were not making a great impression on Andrew. He honestly had no specific advice to give other than his "don't give up" message. Russell knew Andrew didn't leave only because of his respect for him. Russell would have to get his attention.

"God blessed some in my family with *the talent* son. I know many things most people aren't aware of. You've turned your back on friends and family who only have your welfare in mind. Remember, life is a blessing under any circumstance. No matter how bad you think you have it, I can guarantee you someone else has it worse and I know that from experience. I've been where you are right now. I thought long and hard about taking my life as you have. In that moment of despair, I finally saw the *light* that pulled me from the brink. You, Andrew Miller must open your mind to allow yourself to see that l*igh*t so that the same may happen for you."

Andrew seemed to calm down and open his mind to Russell's conversation. "Mr. Russell I can only imagine how difficult it must be to have to suffer through what you've been through, but we're different people and our situations are not the same. I'm reminded every day I look into the mirror and see what I've lost. I can also see pity and hurt on the faces of those who love me. I see their pain, which makes mine worse. My girlfriend at State never came to see me again after they took my bandages off. I have never gotten so much as a Christmas card or heard from her since."

Russell placed his hand on Andrew's and looked him squarely in the eye. "You may have also gained something in this tragedy. Think about who you were and what you really had before this all happened. If you want to relieve the pain you see in the eyes of those who love you, make a resolution to turn this situation around. Find a way and the strength inside yourself (and it is there) to climb out of that dark hole you live in."

At that comment, a song starting playing on the Wurlitzer, *Reaching for the Sky* by Peabo Bryson.

"Listen to that song. The universe sends you messages from many directions son. You only have to listen."

About that time, Mae came over to warm up Russell's coffee and bring Andrew another root beer. "Looks like you fellas are deep in conversation. Can I get you anything else?"

Andrew nodded with a half-smile and she walked back behind the counter. "Look Mr. Russell, I know a little about the history of our town and have heard rumors about you and your family, but I don't need nobody's help to straighten out my life."

Russell thought about what he said and agreed with him. "You're right Andrew. It would be presumptuous of me to even think I could. God leads my feet where they need to be at any given moment. When I saw you coming out the theatre tonight, I knew we needed to talk. I needed to be with you for these brief moments. I will let you go, but before you do, let me look at your right foot."

Andrew gave him a wary look.

"I won't hurt you. This is the one that causes you to limp. Correct?"

Andrew gave him a knowing and suspicious glance, but proceeded to let Russell look.

"The doctors in Jackson told me the bones were broken so badly all they could do was to fuse them together just so I would be able to walk at all." Russell gave a wry smile.

"Take your shoe and sock off for me," he said. Andrew reluctantly did so. Russell took the bare foot (which was slightly crooked and misshapen) in both hands and gently massaged it and just as Andrew released his apprehension, Russell gave the foot a firm and awkward twist.

Andrew heard bones cracking and felt a very sharp, but brief, pain shoot through his entire body. "Ouch," Andrew let out involuntarily and the few patrons who remained all looked in their direction.

"Try that out now. See if the stiffness you had is still there." Andrew shot a serious frown at Russell and then looked at his foot which (to his amazement looked different). It actually looked closer to what it looked like before the accident. He put his sock and shoe on and then put weight on the foot gently at first and then more. It seemed like Russell hadn't broken anything else. As a matter of fact, the foot actually felt a little better. A lot better.

"I'll be right back," he told Russell as he headed toward the restroom. He relieved himself, exited the restroom and headed back to the table. As he walked toward the table, he noticed Russell was no longer there. He also noticed something else. He no longer dragged his foot. It still had some pain from Russell's adjustment, but he was walking with a only a small almost imperceptible limp.

As he neared the table, Ms. Mae approached him. "Russell paid for the bill. Said he had to go. He left a card for you on the table. He said, call him tomorrow."

Andrew could only nod his head toward Miss Mae as he picked up the card and looked at it. It was a simple white card with blue letters. "RUSSELL THOMPSON" -and his title as "Spiritual Advisor & Healer." His telephone number was handwritten in blue ink at the bottom. What was a Spiritual Advisor & Healer? He wasn't sure about any of that mumbo jumbo.

Andrew walked home in perfect stride. His limp, though unnoticed by him was gone by the time he arrived home. He had to admit he felt a little different after his encounter with, this man, Russell Thompson. He spent most of the night tossing and turning trying to digest what Russell had told him and done for him at Mae's Diner.

Andrew's life took an upturn, after his meeting with Russell. When he returned home from work the following Friday, he looked through his mail. There was the usual stuff from the JSU alumni association and junk mail for insurance, but there was also a letter from the Newman Plastic Surgery Reconstructive Institute in New York. It was an invitation to come to New York for an evaluation for entry into an experimental surgery program they were conducting. It was especially designed to treat difficult scars such as the one he had. The Jackson State Athletic Department had submitted his name as a possible candidate for this surgery. He had already endured seven surgeries after the accident. The letter contained before and after photos of the work the institute had performed. Their results were impressive. It looked like the technology had improved vastly since his injury. Though this would be at their expense, he would still have to think about the offer.

Linda noticed the change. She was the first person to notice his limp had disappeared. His pain must also be completely gone since she had not seen any pain medication come via mail over the past three months. Andrew attended Bible study a few weeks in a row and he and Karen seemed to have a lot to talk about afterwards.

Andrew's attitude was different about his life and towards the people in it, after his meeting with Russell Thompson. Andrew now knew Russell was a remarkable person. Russell's perception and wisdom caught him completely off guard. That meeting with Russell actually restored some of his enthusiasm for life.

He had brief conversations with both Linda and Karen about what he would like to do with his life. Karen was a beautiful person and they had become much closer during the past weeks. She was a nice-looking young lady, but his true attraction was her levelheadedness and the sense of calm he felt in her presence. She encouraged him to participate in the experimental surgery. She felt the surgery could possibly sustain the improvement that had already begun in his life.

As the captain was announcing their plane landing from the intercom, he remembered he had never called Mr. Russell after their meeting in Mae's Diner and made a note to do so.

Andrew spent a month recuperating in New York. Linda and Karen were present when the doctor removed his bandages. He could tell from the expressions on their faces there was a significant change. When he peered in the mirror the nurse gave him, he was amazed. The hideous scar on the right side of his face was gone. There was still discoloration where it had been but the doctor silenced his apprehension. "The color will come back in a few weeks and you will be as good as new. We will also fit you with a new prosthetic eye from one of our partners before we release you."

Weeks later, Andrew was back in Thompsonville with many things to be thankful for. He was an older version of his younger self without the attitude. Karen was the best thing that had come into his life. She was so different than the other girls he knew in high school and college. Though other women had started to take notice of him again, Karen was in no danger. There really was something unique about her that even his mother, Linda, recognized when she first met her. Sometimes Moms do pick the best mates for their children, he thought. He and Karen had formed a deep relationship. He was very thankful Mr. Russell had urged him to refocus and see the positives he had around him. In spite of all of the new pluses in his life, Andrew still felt he'd been somewhat short changed in life.

"Andrew, are you sure?" Karen had a very serious look on her face when Andrew offered her the ring. "You barely noticed me when we were in school." Andrew could not argue. He was a star and was always the center of attention for his fellow students (especially the girls). He remembered Karen as quiet and studious but cute in that down home sort of way. She had been faithfully by his side through the past few months of his rehabilitation.

He wondered why he was never attracted to her. "Because you were a different person," she said.

Andrew raised one eyebrow and had a weird thought, *Now you're reading my mind*?

"I am a Thompson" she said. This response gave his face an even more quizzical look. "My mother (Annie Ruth Thompson) married James Arthur Smith, who himself is far removed but still in the Thompson tree. I'm not trying to scare you, but I wasn't sure this day would come for us."

Andrew opened his mouth to speak but Karen but her finger to his lips. "I told my mother when we were in fifth grade I was going to marry Andrew Miller."

"I love you Karen and if that's true what's the problem?" he asked.

"Everybody with the *sight* in Thompsonville is not as well-known as Mr. Russell or his cousin Will. My mother has the real gift of sight among other things. She never said much about you and me until we got serious."

Andrew liked Miss Annie as she was referred to by all in their church. She always had a pleasant smile for him, even after the accident. He had no clue either she or Karen were so much a part of the Thompsonville legacy. For that matter, until he and Mr. Russell talked in Mae's Diner, he wasn't really sure of the significance of the talk and whispers about this town.

"Mom never told me much about you and me but said she wanted to talk to both of us if this day ever came,"Karen continued.

Andrew was still taken aback by the conversation. He knew, in spite of some emotional pain that still lingered, he and Karen were so right for each other.

They had just sat down after a wonderful meal he had at Karen's parent's invitation. His mom Linda was an excellent cook, but Miss Annie's cooking was absolutely off any scale he could think of (especially the peach cobbler). He knew he could never utter that thought out loud to insure his Mom, Linda, never got wind of it.

Mr. Smith conveniently excused himself after the meal to go next door and have a beer and cigar with his friend and fishing buddy, Leroy Sims.

Miss Annie was in her early sixties. She had a beautiful head of completely white hair and was a beautiful woman for her age. She offered Andrew a homebrew and began a serious talk with them both.

"I love my daughter very much and believe your souls may be destined to be together. I believe she's waited her entire life for you. She didn't know I knew this." Karen started to blush. "The universe has a certain flow and some things are meant to be and others are not." Andrew was trying to figure out where this was going. He never envisioned this kind of talk from Miss Annie. "For instance, your accident was exactly that, an accident. You and the other boys who suffered from that terrible mistake probably deserve a second chance." Andrew and Karen both were almost erect in their seats at that comment. Karen had very rarely heard her mom make these type observations or comments and certainly not directly to her or someone close to her. "I believe you and Andrew love each other, but Andrew (among other things) still has some regrets and unresolved issues with his father and brother."

Tears welled in Andrew's eyes as the truth she uttered plunged deeply into his heart. "Those issues would probably be a deterrent to your chances at real happiness."

Karen spoke up. "Are you saying we shouldn't marry each other?" "Not at all. I'm saying you both should allow nature to correct itself," she said.

They each had bewildered looks. Karen knew her Mom had what seemed like supernatural skills and knowledge, but the conversation had now gotten plain strange. She could tell Andrew was thinking the same thing. Miss Annie got up to refill her iced tea and offered Andrew another homebrew which he gladly accepted.

"How could this situation possibly correct itself?" Andrew asked. There's no such thing as time travel," he continued.

"Of course not," Miss Annie added with a wry smile. "Not all knowledge is contained in library books son. The powers that be in this world wouldn't even know where to look for real knowledge. There are things some of us know right here in this town that most of the world will probably never know."

"Tell us more please Miss Annie," Andrew asked.

"Nothing in nature is perfect. You can use basic powers of observation to prove this true. Accidents like the one that took your friend's life and changed your life's direction are errors that can and should be corrected.

"The ancient people who lived here thousands of years before us gained spiritual knowledge and secrets the world of today does not know and would not even believe. Some of this knowledge was gained by certain of us in this family and survives today in our current generation.

"You may be able to re-live that situation and possibly experience a different outcome."

"Time travel?" Andrew asked again.

"No, you hard-head boy," Miss Annie stated in a comical way. "You go back and relive that experience. It's not a back and forth trip like a bus ride. This trip works one way. If you go back, you return to the age and circumstances you were in at a specific time that may give you opportunities to circumvent any unnatural or accidental tragedy. It's like a do over. When you leave this present time, it will cease to exist for you. None of us will remember this conversation (including you) because if you're successful in your journey, today's events will never happen. You will re-live your life with new memories and experiences. Today's conversation and the past years will only be a vague dream that will quickly cease to be a part of yours and anyone else's memory."

Andrew and Karen looked at each other and the looks on their faces asked almost together, "What about us?"

Miss Annie interpreted those looks and the question. "If your love is real and meant to be, you'll find each other, maybe at a different time in your lives, but you will," Annie said. She was very calm and self assured about something that was deathly important to them.

She then left the room and returned with a large book which was in a large plastic bag. She put it on the table and opened it to a page near the end. The writing on the page seemed to be mostly symbols and small handwritten drawings. It was very old and it was not a recognizable language known by either Karen or Andrew. The information Annie was providing was astonishing to her daughter and her beau. She put on her reading glasses and was rapidly scanning the pages she had located. "It says this must be done on a night with a full moon. It must be done at any of six locations identified in our part of the world." Miss Annie recognized the landmarks and figured the closest location to be only about ten miles away near the Choctaw Indian Reservation.

That was a strange night for Andrew and Karen. They agreed to talk this issue over and let Miss Annie know if Andrew would be open to try this spell. Andrew thought it couldn't hurt but what if it worked and he and Karen lost each other forever. He knew the chance to set things right with his brother and father and to save his friends was something he deeply wanted. He was already a changed person inside now. He cared about someone other than himself. He could now see and appreciate the positive things in himself and others. Would he still be that way after he went back or would he be the somewhat self-centered and selfish person he was before his accident? Would he remember anything about Karen and himself? He could tell she was as apprehensive as he was. Would any of this stuff really work? He had to at least give it a try. He had no choice. He also owed that to Sammy and Swill.

November 14th was the evening of the full moon. Andrew, Miss Annie and Karen had reached the calculated spot at exactly 9:00pm. They came quite a way down a dark dirt road. It was there on the banks of the Pearl River that Miss Annie pointed to the exact spot and asked Andrew to stand there.

She retrieved items from her bag and immediately began what sounded like an Indian chant and moved chakra beads all around Andrew. She tossed ashes and bird feathers in an elliptical circle all around him. Though the moonlight shone through the trees, it was very dark in the woods. Karen held a candle near so Miss Annie could read the script of the spell. Andrew was standing very still facing the large sandbar in the river. He was first apprehensive about Karen and Miss Annie being left alone in the dark woods if and after he departed. If this spell actually worked, (according to Miss Annie) this would be a reality that would never be.

The woods seemed to glow with a faint light at first, then got brighter as a circular portal of bluish light that formed to Miss Annie's left side slowly opened. When it was fully formed, she pointed for Andrew to enter while continuing her strange chant and motions around him. Her eyeballs rolled up into her head as she continued her chant. He looked in fear and awe at the portal and took one last loving look at Karen. He cautiously, at Miss Annie's urging, stepped through the portal.

The noise was deafening. The bright lights all around left him slightly dazed until he realized he was standing on the five yard line in Thompsonville High football stadium field in his high school football uniform, complete with pads and helmet. He could feel youthful strength in his body and the rush of blood through his veins as he looked up just in time to see the laces on the football slowly rotating as it dropped into his arms. With a jolt, he remembered what is was like to see using both eyes. He instinctively cradled the ball and made a quick dart cut, which set up his blocks on the left side perfectly. He broke through the initial wall of pursuit, put a move on number fifty-five for Lanier High and flat outran their kicker on his way to a ninety-five yard return for a touchdown.

The cheering of the crowd was deafening. Their opposing kickoff team had really underestimated his quickness and foot speed. He entered the end zone and gave the ball to the referee then headed to the sidelines to be mobbed by his teammates. Andrew had really been mentally confused lately. He scored with a minute left in the game which gave Thompsonville a ten point lead and put the game on ice. That is the only part of the game he clearly remembered. He remembered this game was really important. A win guaranteed THS a spot in the 1963 Big 10 South playoffs. Andrew felt like there was something he needed to remember that was just below the surface of his mind. Well, never mind. He showered and dressed and waved briefly at Coach Billups on his way out of the gym. "Great game Miller. This game will surely get you that offer from J State," the coach said.

Marlon Thompson came up to him to let him know. "Andrew, your girl is waiting for you outside." This was a little confusing. He was slightly disturbed because for a second, he couldn't remember having a girlfriend. As he exited the gym, there in the middle of the crowd was a sixteen year-old, soon to be seventeen years, Karen Smith, who was looking at him as if he were the only other person in the world. She was beautiful in every way. His heart fluttered as he met her gaze. Then he remembered. How could he forget? They had gone to the prom together last year. They hugged and shared a brief kiss. The uncomfortable knot eased in his stomach and everything seemed right in the world. He would walk her home as he did after each home game and then get back so he, Dad and Eli could have hot cocoa and talk about the details of tonight's game.

SHADE TREE WILLIE
(1962)

Just outside Mae's Diner across the street from Mr. Ezra's country store was the town square. It was a small park with a statue of Dora Jane Thompson in its center. She was the matriarch of the all-Black town of Thompsonville. Dora Jane was the Moses who freed her family of Georgia slaves, but did not live to see their Mississippi promised land. Only in her visions did she see this peaceful oasis for her kin. The park in her honor was now a place for folks of the town to rest, fellowship and take in Thompsonville's peaceful setting. The large oak tree at the West end of the park was home to the crew of older Black men. These fellows were retired, disabled, no longer working or those who just stopped by to chat and get the latest news (including gossip).

Some played checkers, some played chess or just quietly read newspapers or magazines. Most participated off and on in the all day conversations and heated discussions that were always centered under "Mama Dora's" large oak tree.

The weather was good most days of the year. Midsummer days were hot. There was a late arriving crowd at the park during those hot afternoons. Cold weather and rain were the only things that provided the regular park crew its infrequent days off.

"I tell you Ernie Davis won't be better than Jim Brown" Ralph Stinger said.

"If they think he won't then why is they paying him $100,000?" asked Pete Barnes. These old timers loved their football.

"What y'all don't see coming," Ralph continued, "is the end of good Negro college football. All of the youngsters coming up now that can really play will start going to White schools like Ole Miss and LSU. J State and Alcorn won't be able to touch good Negro players anymore."

The group thought about this for a while. "Now I'll believe that when I see it," replied Ezra Johnson who normally ate his sandwich with the old timers at lunch time.

"Man, have you seen this week's centerfold in Jet?" asked Leroy Spade. Many of the group of the men quickly gathered around him as he opened the magazine lengthwise to a chorus of wolf whistles and "ummhmmms" uttered by the group.

"She don't look better than Lena Horne," one man scoffed.

"Amen to that," another one chimed in.

"You boys ought to be trying to get your souls right. All of y'all getting close to the finish line," said Henry Thompson one of the deacons of St. Paul's Baptist Church.

That comment prompted quiet murmurs and groans of displeasure. They knew what was coming next. Some of the most heated discussions held around the big oak were about religion. You could tell the oak tree group didn't really want to get into a prolonged discussion on that subject today. Deacon Henry was a young man, by their standards (barely fifty years old), who rarely came out to the park. When he did, he usually brought some drama with him.

Leroy was not really a church going man and he loved asking the deacon questions that made him squirm. He was just about to pose one at that moment when someone else beat him to it. "Deacon Henry. You don't really believe it's a sin to look at the centerfold in Jet magazine, do you?" asked Pete Thompson.

These were morally strict times everywhere in America. "It is sinful to look at a woman in lust," Deacon Henry countered. "Well, I spent my twenty cents on this Jet and I'll be gall durned if I ain't gwine look at every page and that includes the centerfold," Leroy replied in an exaggerated tone.

Muffled chuckling rose from the group. With that response, Deacon Henry looked sternly at Leroy, tipped his hat to the group and walked away.

"Thank the Lord for small blessings" Pete Thompson stated. All were glad to see the disapproving Deacon Henry make a hasty exit. Most of the oak tree regulars attended church, but, none were happy about being called out as sinners.

"Willie, you always quiet when religious talk starts," said Leroy.

Shade Tree Willie Patterson was a venerable member of the group. He was revered and respected by all in the park. He was their local chess master. He had spent twenty-five years in the military. He lived and worked in Chicago after retiring from the military. He moved back to Thompsonville a few years back after his wife passed away. He was now a daily fixture in the park. As he contemplated his next chess move, he actually provided a response to Leroy's comment which surprised everyone. "Nothing for me to discuss," he replied. With that response, everything in the park got quiet. Even Duke Thompson's dog Pee Wee, opened one eye and tiredly stared at Willie. In an unofficial park vote two years ago, Pee Wee won hands down as the laziest dog in Thompsonville.

"Don't practice it," said Willie. Everybody was amazed not only at Willie joining in the conversation, but also at what he said. Willie wore freshly pressed denim overalls every day. He was clean shaven, wore horn rimmed glasses and still had most of his thick gray hair. Even with his Chicago Cubs baseball cap, he was resplendent in the "uniform of the day" for the Thompsonville "Oak Tree Crew." One moment after his comment, he turned away from Slim (his chess opponent) to address the group's further questions.

"You don't believe in a higher power"" Ralph Stinger inquired.

"Of course, I do. What fool doesn't?" Willie replied.

"Dere's a lot of dem there atheists out dere," said Duke Thompson. "And dey don't believe in nuthin."

Willie sat quietly staring at Duke for a moment. His expression gave no clue as to what his response would be. Finally, he stated. "No, I'm no atheist." You could almost hear the wheels turning in their heads as many had finally gotten something they had longed for; a rise out of Shade Tree Willie.

Willie knew this conversation was going to come eventually. He knew he was an enigma to most of the Oak Tree Crew and probably to most folks in Thompsonville. Many points of view were held in the park regarding politics, religion, sin, heaven and hell and the like. He had heard most yet never looked up from the chess board to add his two cents.

Leroy got between Willie and the group. "You fellas know Willie. He's family. He grew up with us and he's one of the few of us who's been anywhere and done a few things. We should respect his right to his privacy."

Willie raised his hand ever so slightly to acknowledge his appreciation for Leroy's attempt to deflect the conversation away from him. "'Scuse me Slim," said Willie to his favorite chess partner, "We can pick this match up later."

He was now completely turned around facing the group. It was finally the day for Shade Tree Willie to hold court under the big oak tree in Dora Jane Park.

"True Roy, I was born and raised right here in Thompsonville. Joined the army right out of high school. I served in WWII and spent twenty-five years in the military. I've been to all forty-eight, excuse me, to forty-eight of the fifty states. I went to school with you and Duke and played baseball with some of you in high school. I attended Sunday School most weeks at St. Paul before Deacon Henry was even born." There was a lot of "uh huh's" and affirmative nodding of the heads at his comments.

He continued, "I have been quiet in many of the conversations that go on under this tree." The audience was captivated since these were as many words as any of them had ever heard from Willie's mouth during his time under the tree. Because he was a Thompsonville native, he seemed to get along with almost everyone. He seemed to really enjoy being a member of the tribe.

"I do believe there is a guiding force that directs each and every one of our lives. Let me tell you about what happened to me a few years back. I've been a lot of places but, I had an experience that changed me forever." The group was getting a real treat today. Willie continued to speak. He did not come off as an egotistical or vain man. His voice was clearly audible and though he did not speak very loud, its tone captured the undivided attention of the group. "Because of that, I no longer consider myself Baptist, Methodist, Lutheran, Catholic, Muslim or a member of any religion."

Okay, what he said just now moved the comfort level of the group to another place. Willie, who was smart enough to realize that fact raised his hand briefly and continued above the murmurs. “Let me be clear. Some of you know I was raised in the church right alongside most of you. I’m not trying to convert anybody to the way I think. I am only going to tell you a story about something that happened to change me. Whether you believe it or not won't change me one way or the other. Those of you who wonder why I get involved in certain discussions, may get your answer today”.

Ralph interrupted him. “You were a member of the 92nd Infantry Division in the war. True? The Buffalo Soldiers?”

“True, we saw combat in Italy, but what I’m going to tell you happened after my time in World War II,” he replied. “Fellas, let's don't get off the subject,” he continued in that cool way.

“Something profound happened to me twelve years ago in Chicago. I had just retired from military service two years earlier and had a pretty good job working for Chicago Transit as a bus mechanic. Between the pay I got there and my army retirement, me and Hattie Mae did pretty good. Chicago was, and still is, a good place for Negroes to make a living. I caught the L Train everyday to get to work. One day after I stopped at the corner vendor cart to get my coffee and the latest Chicago Defender, I started walking across the street toward the bus barn. I guess my mind was drifting a little as I peeked the headlines and sipped my coffee. The next thing I know, I hear this loud noise and I’m sent flying, newspaper blowing in all different directions, coffee all over me and I was basically knocked senseless.

“The next thing I know, I wake up in Cook County General.

Hattie Mae and Lillie, our Daughter, are at my bedside and I have this huge bandage on my head. I couldn't move my right side. Hattie Mae told me my right hip was broken and I had a bad bump on my head. Doctor said it was only a slight skull fracture, but my head was hurting some bad. Hattie Mae said my accident happened three days before. They were just happy to see me wake up. Man, I was in a lot of pain but, I knew I must be some kind of lucky to still be alive. All of those years in the army and I didn't get so much as a scratch and I get knocked clean out of my shoes crossing 74th Street in Chicago.

My memories of what happened started to become clear after a few days. I actually remember hearing someone far in the distance pronounce me dead at 10:51am in the hospital emergency room.

I began to remember everything that happened to me in the smallest detail. It was as real as if it was happening right now. I was told I still had a faint heartbeat when they got me to the emergency room, but my heart stopped after that for a five full minutes."

Ezra Johnson suddenly interjected, "If you was gone that long, you must have had what they call a near death experience".

Willie acknowledged Ezra's comment with a nod. Ezra was a brother who was pretty well read and versed in many subjects.

"Exactly, at least that's what the doctor said I probably had." By that time, another question arose from Leroy, "What was it like? Did you see anybody you know?"

"Whoa" said Willie. "I wasn't in the land of milk and honey and I didn't see Mama or Daddy or the ancestors. Nobody was there to meet me. I truly believe I got a look at the other side." Now with that, all of the group was waiting for him to continue. Willie could see the questions etched on their faces. He replied this way. "No, I didn't see any White people. I also didn't see any Black folk. For that matter, there were no people at all, no animals, no water, no sky or green grass; none of that."

That statement created puzzled looks all around. Willie was known as a quiet man, but the consensus look on the faces of the group said, *This Negro sure can spin a tale.* He picked up on this but did not react in any way.

"After the impact with the truck, I felt weightless. I no longer had a body. I was made of light. I felt myself floating and rising. The higher I rose, the closer I moved toward the Source. The Source was a huge light that had *consciousness* like me, that I could sense and feel. It was very bright and so pure and strong. It was huge and had no limit. It was too bright and too pure for me. I felt I would only rise as far as I could stand. Right then, I felt better than I ever had during my entire life. The closer I got to that source, the better I felt. There were many other lights like me in every direction. They were above me, below me and to either side of me. Some were ascending, some were descending and some were stationary. I finally stopped rising and remained stationary. My being could not tolerate any more of the purity or the brightness of the light. I was where I was supposed to be and it felt so good. I had no needs. The Source gave me all I needed. I felt no hunger, thirst or any

other physical need. As I already said, I had no body.

Neither did those all around me. I was as aware of them as I am aware of all of you. I was at peace. I never wanted to be anyplace other than where I existed at that moment. Time did not pass. I felt so good and had no other need than what I received from the light. I could have stayed right there forever. Past and future were no more. All that existed was NOW. What I felt within me and all around me was love.

"All the others were like me, (existing only to receive and give love to each other and receive from the Source). Some light beings felt very familiar. It was as if we had known each other in some other life or some other place or situation. Although there were many I had no prior recognition, we all shared love and light between us. There was no distinction of sex, wealth, color or anything else that we use to identify ourselves as human beings. There was only the "I am" or "I exist" that connected us.

"If you can imagine how good any of you felt at anytime in your life or if you can imagine how somebody must feel who is high, intoxicated, or under the influence; if somebody could take that feeling and multiply it times ten thousand, it wouldn't even come close to how good I felt."

Willie let his boys digest the magnitude of this statement. "When you think about it, everything we do as human beings (to one degree or another) in life is meant to make us feel good. The difference is, none of what we have as living beings on this Earth is permanent. Think about it. We must come down from every high. We eventually run out of time, good looks, money or many of the other things that give our lives pleasure; they all fade away or we run short of them or no longer receive the same satisfaction they gave us in the beginning. Junkies, alcoholics or other drug users are all examples of those who use shortcuts to receive the good feelings we all seek. Of course, these people eventually lose meaningful things like health or social standing, which dulls the initial satisfaction they got when they started out. They find that the path they've been on is a quick dead end."

Willie was laying down some serious knowledge and the group was keenly trying to absorb the words he spoke.

Finally Ezra asked a poignant question. "If that was real and as good as you say it was, why didn't you stay there?"

Willie's face gave a look that said, *somebody is listening*. "Ezra, I can only guess it was just not my time. Ever so slightly, my light started to fade, and I found myself descending and going further away from the light. I was falling slowly at first and then faster until I was at the bottom. The sudden shock forced me to open my eyes. There I was in a hospital bed. Hattie Mae was holding my hand. As I regained my senses, the pain in my hip, head and almost my entire body came back with a vengeance. I actually almost cried out in pain. The nurse brought this big needle with as the biggest dose of morphine they were allowed to give me. It eased the pain tremendously."

Pete asked the next obvious question. "You sure dem drugs wasn't the reason for that light show you was gettin?"

His question got a few muffled chuckles and "Amen's" from the group. All could see Willie was not moved from his conviction that what he took was indeed a spiritual journey. "That big shot of morphine gave me no kick like what I felt for the time I was near the source. It only dulled the pain I felt. I also know a few other things. I am a changed man inside after that. It took me just about nine months to fully recover from the injuries of my accident. Even before my health came back, I felt a peace inside that I still feel today. This is even after Hattie Mae passed away two years later.

"I feel something and have something I never felt or had before that accident. We all know everybody has a time. That was not my time, but maybe it was a peek into what this all is, what it was and what it will truly be. Who knows? Maybe the supreme being just wanted me to stick around to give my testimony to each of you."

The group was totally dumbfounded. You could tell nobody was expecting Willie to talk on this particular subject. "I no longer worry about what going to happen to me when I leave this place. I also know the good I do in life brings me closer to that feeling I felt in that magnificent light. The bad things move me further away. That was a lesson I believe we all know deep inside and now I can't help but try to practice it each day I live. All things like religion, having more money than I can spend, driving a big car, being rich and famous no longer hold much attraction for Willie T. Patterson. Peace, light and love are now real things that I will always believe in because I think I've had a firsthand look at the TRUE Almighty. To be here with you guys in the park each day, is as good as it gets for an old timer like me. Now if y'all will excuse me, Slim and I still have a match to finish."

Drop the mic!! It was if someone had snapped their fingers and the entire group was awakened from a hypnotic spell.

After that statement, Ezra Johnson looked at his pocket watch and said, "Man, it's 1:30. I need to get back to the store." Pete, Duke and Pee Wee slowly ambled toward Mae's to get the lunch special. Leroy Spade, Ralph and some of the other men quietly moved back to their checker games. Others went back to reading their newspapers and magazines on the park benches. For those brief moments, a weighty silence reigned under the big oak tree in Dora Jane Park. One thing was for sure, after that afternoon, nobody ever asked Shade Tree Willie his opinion on anything.

ABOUT THE AUTHOR

Otis Windham Jr. is a first time author of fiction. Many of the short stories presented in this work were written and rewritten over a period of the last twenty years. He is a southerner who was born and raised in the segregated south. He grew up during the Civil Rights Movement and like most of the generation in that era benefited from the gains of the struggle.

His interest as a serious writer of fiction was powered by creative writing skills he originally learned and developed during his undergraduate years at Jackson State college in Mississippi. He did not pick up his interest in serious writing again until his early forties. He has written numerous magazine and newspaper articles on various sports and travel themes.

Thompsonville Collection Mystic Song of the South is mostly a product of his childhood and his young adult recollections and experiences. He is the father of three sons (all Aquarians), one daughter (Gemini) and three grandsons and one granddaughter. He is a member of the Orlando Renaissance Writer's Guild and a member of the Vulcan Golf Club, which outside of golfing, contribute to the wellbeing and development of their community through charitable giving and events. He is currently retired and living in Birmingham, Alabama.